ALARMING HEAT

ALARMING HEAT

by
Regine Sands

Boston • Lace Publications
an imprint of Alyson Publications, Inc.

Acknowledgments:
Thank Heaven for Christina,
my thorough and thoroughly gorgeous editor,
and Charles for his overwhelming generosity

Also by Regine Sands:
   Travels with Diana Hunter

Typeset and printed in the United States of America.

This is an original paperback from Lace Publications,
an imprint of Alyson Publications, Inc.,
40 Plympton St., Boston, Mass. 02118.

Distributed in England by GMP Publishers,
P.O. Box 247, London N17 9QR England.

First edition, first printing: May 1991

5 4 3 2 1

ISBN 1-55583-311-X

To Christina Louise.
You are everything to me.
Every single little thing.

Contents

Georgia Marks

She puts on the blue sharkskin pants; shiny, narrow, cool. A crisp white shirt follows, and loafers spit-polished. Bold sterling jewelry — silent silver statements. Already Georgia is attitude.

She tries on two ties, two bolos. She chooses the more masculine of the quartet. She slicks back her hair, rejects the makeup, turns smile to smirk. Fresh, almost there, almost boy.

The phone rings for the millionth time tonight. It's Ian or Sara. She turns the music up louder. Leaves both lovers behind. Time to drive.

In a minute Pacific Highway 1 is beneath her black tires, the entire Pacific Ocean hers. She's driving very fast.

Expanding, metamorphosing. She'll soon be boy, soon.

On the prowl, a cannibal of a queer lust. She won't rest tonight until she casts out her reel and snares her prey.

Minutes later Georgia's overheating. *Georgia wants what Sara gives her, but doesn't want Sara, wants what Ian gives her, but doesn't want Ian.*

She pulls into the rest stop on the side of the cliff, kills the lights and engine, and unzips her trousers.

Fingers in her pants, on her cunt — she loves the curve of it, the damp of it — giving praise roughly. No pretense or pretty talk, no fondling or foreplay.

She wants sex. Sex without subtext.

Wants it now, in the dark auto with her back against the car door and her pants pushed beneath her cunt. She talks to herself, tells herself to do it. Georgia, your fingers are there, poised, impatient. *Boys don't wait, what are you waiting for?* She opens the glove compartment.

Dark hair, dark night, dark desire.

With her thumb and index finger she parts the mat of hair to get to the lips of her pussy. She turns it on, slips the vibrator in between.

Georgia is easy access, moist and open.

In a girl fist she holds the cold thing like she's gotta have it.

She lifts her tense body off the seat. A strong hand slides the stiff thing inside her, another pushes the trousers below her ass. She lowers her ass to the leather. She wants to keep her clothes on and she wants to rip her clothes off. Her fingers rub, enlarge everything they touch. Her forearms harden, likewise her clit.

Already it's obvious it's too easy too fast. She'll come in a flash.

No. The girl in her seizes control, slows it down.

She half leans, half lies across both front bucket Saab seats. The steering wheel takes up valuable space.

Georgia bears down hard on the hard thing inside her. She lifts her thighs, parts them, expands the passage into her pussy. Her fingers slow, stroking her clit lightly, hips pulling back and pushing forward, also slow.

Fingers spread her lips apart so Georgia can watch herself in the act.

Her pussy changes color when she's aroused, Sara showed her that.

Her lips swell with the fresh blood, double their size. Her vagina opens wide letting anything that wants in, in.

Georgia finds her rhythm.

Her hair, oiled back, falls loose, long and sensual against her neck where Sara spilled so many kisses.

The boy in her uncages the animal within. She's alone. She doesn't have to lie about it, just feed it.

The vibrator sinks into her. It sends a rolling resonance into the echo chamber of her vagina. Her hips rise to meet it, push up against it, then release. She pauses. She dips the shivering steel inside her, sweeping it between slick lips. She hears her wetness when her sex sucks up the vibrator.

She feels the back of her starched shirt sticking to her skin. She feels the weight of the vibrator, perfectly balanced in her palm. *And she feels the boy rushing her.*

Georgia moves the fingers of her free hand to explore her asshole. Her aroma changes, it grows more potent so her scent can be picked up from a distance.

Her sweating body works hard, sends its best energy to her groin. Her legs are two steel rubber bands, athlete's legs.

The muscles in her cunt quiver with the buzzing, grasp the slippery thing, hold it, let it go. Expert muscles.

If it were a cock — Ian's cock — it'd be rock hard by now. Her hand pushes it in. Her body twists in response, embraces it.

She's making love to herself, feeling the power of it.

Girl turned boy turns tigress. Like a cat she gets up on all fours. Her hair falls forward, covers her face. She lowers her head to the seat, rests a wet cheek against the warm leather. Her ass is in the air. On her knees Georgia growls with the heat escaping between her legs. Pants down around her knees, ass and sex exposed. She returns the vibrator to her vagina. Like sculling, strong clean movements. Pumping arms and shoulders glistening with sweat.

Hot boy, hot girl sounds in Georgia's throat.

It could have been Ian fucking her, they were his clothes she was wearing. It could have been Sara teasing her asshole, it was Sara's jewelry she had on.

Blue eyes can't see, her hair blocks their view of the grand Pacific. There is no more public place in the world for her to do what she's doing. So brave, exposed under the infinite horizon of stars and sea.

Legs tucked up under her chest, the vibrator resonating with a capital R, drilling its point home between her thighs. Georgia rocks back and forth on the heated leather seats knowing she's going to make herself explode with the orgasm.

She pushes the unfeeling thing inside her vagina as deeply as it will go. Her scent is inviting, her cunt, all-welcoming. Soaked, open, blood red. Her hand works the steel still deeper into her bottomless cunt. She can feel the steel tip tingling, titillating her cervix. She can feel her muscles tighten around it, sucking it in, holding it there. She can feel the void when the muscles of her vagina relax and the lips of her cunt open and expel it. Like dancing, like music, like the tides ebb and flow, her greedy mouth pulling it all the way in then pushing it all the way out ... Yes, of course Georgia can take it. Take it in one swallow if she had to. Both lovers had shown her how.

No sweet nothings, nothing fancy tonight. Her other hand grabs at the edge of the bucket seat to pull her body free from the vibrator, then to push her body down onto it. Muscles taut then slack. Vibrator in then out. An isometric fuck. Georgia's sweating.

Oh, the heady scent of her come. Dry lips from labored breathing, the cat-in-heat licks her lips and purrs. Windows steaming.

Every single muscle tenses and releases in this magnificent sexual encounter. Her fingertips can't help agitating the tiny kiss curls around her cunt ... fingers doing their job, rousing ... familiar twitching, unfamiliar tingling, a restless clit unsteady beneath the buzzing vibrato and the rough rhythm of rubbing ... turbulent tremors and her vagina spasms beneath the squeezing muscles ... hips writhing, hips squirming and pressing back against the steel ... cunt colliding with the reverberating thing ... vibrator held firm in an insistent fist ... fist smacking against her insolent ass raised high ... with each sweet stroke her fist bumps up against her butt ... but momentum's got her now, momentum pitches her body forward on the car seat, body braced for the orgasm ... she makes a foolish last stand and resists but keeps burying the shivering thing inside her ... keeps the orgasm at arm's length but keeps immersing it into her soaking cunt ...

beats it back until she no longer can ... fingers return to her clit ... she can't wait ... fingers stroking ... can't wait ... fingers rubbing ... can't possibly wait...

An unruly lust grips her. Her clitoris throbs, heart beats hard, frantic like madmen. Her muscles from her waist down freeze. A flash flood of lust mounts, makes its way from the mouth of her vagina. A beautiful and savage turbulence grips her cunt. She lurches forward on the car seat.

Such a strenuous ardor when boy meets girl inside Georgia.

She zips her fly, tucks in her shirt, slicks back her hair, drops the vibrator on the seat next to her.

The smell of her sex on her fingers; an inspired gift to herself between her legs. She starts the engine. November sixth, the birthday girl's forty today.

Natalie & Clare

*A*ll eyes turn to the aurora borealis. Natalie drops her hand to my thigh. I lower my eyes to the palm melting my 50ls. I love the girl so much it makes my stomach hurt. The light above and her hand below make my loins sizzle.

It was my idea to cut class, and Natalie's to come to the planetarium. We're at home in the dark, like two secrets.

It's no surprise that she starts in. "From the back row, Clare, we've got the southwest corner of the place practically to ourselves."

"I don't like public sex, sugar," I say, sweet but tart, *"I don't like public anything."* But I'm not blind, I see the great restlessness flow through her. I can't expect her to sit with it for long. "Half empty," I stress, like it's going to make a difference, "isn't the same thing as empty—"

"And an hour's not the same thing as an afternoon!" All emotion. Everything with Natalie is right now, life and death, passion and more passion. We're very different 23-year-olds with nothing and everything in common. That's what makes it work. That's what makes it hot.

"SECOND IN ORDER FROM THE SUN, THE PLANET OF LOVE AND BEAUTY..."

Venus is projected on the domed ceiling screen. A whole planet (like my whole life) devoted to love. The *yes* pulls at me and the *no* presses on me and I feel my excitement surface as it always does when Natalie demands some sacrifice. *Still, I'm a girl who needs her privacy,* I tell myself. I whisper my "No," weakly.

Natalie's parents are in sales in New York and naturally a *no* means little to them. It means *nothing* to Natalie. Angry silver bangles, a dozen of them, sound their protest when she moves her hand to the crotch of my jeans.

She's a sculptress and I'm her model — that's how we met last month. And right from day one she told me that her need for me *"feels like lightning between my legs"* and that *"it hurts to hold it in."* She leaves no breathing space between wanting me and taking me, and nothing else on earth *but me* will do! It's hard not to let this kind of talk get to you.

"It's a *thirty*-minute star show and we've got *less than sixty minutes* before our next class." Natalie underscores the math, just in case I can't tell time or something. And then she grabs me and kisses me on the mouth, to coerce the *yes* out of me. The wide-open warmness of her mouth envelopes ... then overwhelms me. It disrupts the flow of things inside me. I'm good for nothing when it comes to Natalie's kissing. I return the kiss, or rather, it pours out of me. My lips are more than willing, my tongue follows hers everywhere. I keep my gray eyes shut so I can see Natalie's fleshy hips, thighs, and those better-to-bury-myself-in breasts. I slide into a fast heat and it shows. My lips suck in hers, my lips lick everything in sight. Wet love, free love. My tongue rushes into the sleek, velvet slipperiness of her mouth where she drinks in my saliva like spring water. *This is no giddy, girly, dainty kiss.*

On the other side of the auditorium are four dozen high schoolers on a science class outing. They couldn't be making more noise. But it's dead silent in the eye of this lovestorm where I'm lost somewhere in Natalie.

"AN AERIAL VIEW OF THE PLANET EARTH REVEALS NO NATURAL BOUNDARY LINES..."

At the ten-minute mark Natalie withdraws her lips and gives me that look. There is no use pretending that I don't know that "she-has-gotta-have-me-or-she'll-just-die" look.

"Say yes, Clare."

"I don't see the charm of public sex." But who am I kidding — I'm obviously addicted to the girl. So I say, "Yes, sugar, yes," because with Natalie yes is always the right answer. And because I've never said no to her.

Natalie breaks into that winning smile of hers. In her white t-shirt, baggy denims worn through below her ass and knees, and her dusty green cowboy boots pointy to a fault, Natalie's a Midwestern archetype. I prepare myself to be fucked publicly by a cowgirl.

Smoothly, Natalie unbuckles my leather belt and unbuttons the five 501 buttons. Brazenness is becoming on her. Together we softly, quietly wrestle with the denim. I push my jeans to my knees and Natalie pulls them down to my ankles. I ease my body down in my seat and then my crazy lover eases my thighs apart.

"MARS, CONSPICUOUS FOR THE REDNESS OF ITS LIGHT..."

I feel her obsession for me on her fingertips, like possessing me will make me hers forever. Natalie's fingers with their big need touch my naked skin for the first time. My thighs come alive. Cold fingers caress and I respond at once with a green light. "Set your fingers free, sugar." And even though it goes without saying, I say it because she likes to hear it.

Natalie lays claim to every reachable inch of my down-covered legs like she might miss something, god forbid. "Fifteen minutes come and gone," she whispers, like it's my fault.

"JUPITER, GOD OF LIGHT, THE SKY, AND WEATHER..."

It's too dark to see, so all other senses spring to life. I don't believe in perfume or panties — my own scent is strong and wonderful. Natalie inhales the fragrance too. I watch her hand as it's drawn toward the birthplace of that scent, the place where my skin trembles.

A row of five obnoxious teens are ushered back out into the daylight. Their schoolmates cheer. I feel finger-nails creating friction up the insides of my thighs. I sit very still like something depends on it. Sure enough with a calm quietness, with an "Ahh" from Natalie, her finger-tips connect with my cunt. I ache aloud at the contact and a fast hand covers my mouth.

"Calm down," from Natalie.

"Quiet down," from the front row.

Then we giggle madly. But Natalie's right, I've got to be perfect in my silence. "Sorry," I say and I mean it. She wants to know, "How sorry?" I spread my thighs wider, "Sorry enough?" I stay out of her way — I focus on the narrator's drone and watch the Dog Star formation above. But facts and figures are wasted on me. I can't concentrate on anything but Natalie's palm on my pussy. I like this private-public-Planetarium-sex business. *I like it a lot.*

So does Natalie. Her fingertips are savoring my lips.

My cream makes for smooth sailing along the edge of my overstimulated cunt. Slick lips covered in transluscent cream. I feel the fountain between my legs.

At the eighteen-minute mark the audience breaks into spontaneous applause and I look up to the screen but nothing's there. I missed it, whatever it was, *and I don't care.*

Natalie wets her fingers and returns them to my lap. She hesitates (strategy planning, no doubt), then presses her fingertips against the rim of my vagina to moisten it with her saliva. Natalie's fingers travel around the tiny perimeter with a tender persuasion, a kind persistence. She waits as long as it takes for my cunt to open fully. Only in sex does she have the patience of a lesbian saint. A great wetness awaits her there inside me, but I let her find that out for herself.

Natalie slides her finger into my vagina. From my waist up, no one would guess. I feel her single finger within me. She is inside my body. My movement's inevitable and, thankfully, invisible in the dark. I'm unprepared for the ambush of emotions imploding somewhere in my rib cage. All of a sudden, I want to undo my shirt and expose myself completely to this moment.

Natalie slips a second finger between the petal lips of my cunt. I am so unfuckingbelievably excited by the stealth. Natalie's touch is endearing in its refusal to rush. Her mind and heart race but not her hand. I'm grateful for the slowness. Natalie's gratitude simply can't be put into words. With ten minutes remaining, Natalie steals into my vagina again and again with love-slicked fingers.

All at once I'm mesmerized, her captive audience, titillated, exhilarated. This dark seduction eclipses my reason, and logic takes a backseat to lust. I can't conceal my rapture when she enters me again, more deeply. And again. *I know what she is after.* I let the secret fuck begin.

We both gravitate toward the orgasm like we're hypnotized...

My sighs sift through the air above me but they're overshadowed by the booming Mahler orchestral. The Ninth Symphony. Meteor showers rain down on me from the dome screen. The incandescence is my heart splitting open with feelings for Natalie. My thighs shiver with the tender thrusting. The weakness spreads. *I am pure cream.*

Natalie's fingers penetrate. They rub against the resilient muscles, skim the walls of my cunt awash in come for her. And little by little, Natalie increases the pressure until she feels the birth of my arousal on her fingertips. Then she pulls out, denying me this orgasm. Natalie feels reckless — eight minutes remain. "I'm going to turn you into an exhibitionist yet."

She threatens me with it, like it hasn't already happened. "Go on then, sugar, spoil me." I rear up my hips and Natalie climbs inside me, inside the dark pool, inside the smooth smoothness of me, the hot-as-hell heat of me, the sweet sticky liquid of me. I'm all over her fingers, dripping down into the palm of her hand where she can feel it and taste it and do whatever she wants with it. One finger, then two, now three ... And I, a girl for whom faster's better, pick up speed. I press my hips down on her fingers. *I don't have eight minutes*, I don't want to wait. The thought of waiting is intolerable. The thought of Natalie not taking me in a big, noisy, hungry way provokes me. I'm baffled by the sudden velocity of my own desire. There's a fever in my cunt and only one thing will do. I'm straightforward. *"Eat me."*

"Not here, Clare, I can't." Natalie's surprised and delighted.

I insist. *"I can't wait."* I'm not joking. *"Please."* The orgasm due me lurks in the shadows knowing it's only a matter of time. Six minutes, to be exact. My cream is being passed between us and there's seemingly no end to it. I can't stare into the infinity of space above me anymore. My lips are burnt-red with readiness. *My orgasm wants out.*

"THOROUGHLY DISPUTED TIBETAN INFORMATION INDICATING THE EXISTENCE OF 115 PLANETS..."

Through sheer willpower I hold my hips still. But my deliberate stillness is thick with need. Natalie's watching me closely. She tells me what she sees. "You're gorgeous under the weight of an orgasm. Your red lips are like your cunt ... opening ... waiting to be penetrated." She sculpts my orgasm with whispers and touches. She caresses my clitoris first hard next soft, then fast then slow, then long then short. I am light-headed. She whispers so low now that I hear only the outline of her words, but what does the content matter? On the ceiling a ship makes its way across space and *I* am the dark expanse into which the spaceship voyages. I open further to Natalie.

Natalie leans over, giving me the go-ahead. She exhales a single breath across my clit. *I am a waterfall.* Only a minute left. She reads my mind, she prompts me. *"It's time to let go now."*

I dive into it headfirst. It's a burning hotheaded orgasm, wild, fearless, indiscreet. I grab the armrests and hold on as the release ripples through me. Wave after wave of tiny tremors wash against my cunt, race through me, run right over me. The restrained strain of my orgasm, a secret suffering, is unendurable. I'm dying for her kiss. Stray strands of hair stick to my lips. I feel fingers diving into the depths of me, following the currents of my stream to their source. Natalie's fingers persevere like she's got her mind set on seconds. There's no time, no energy for a second wind. I am hard hit. I've got to stretch my legs, extend my body, curse, thrash, kiss, call out Natalie's name again and again and *Love*, I've got to scream, *Love me, Natalie.* But I don't.

A sweet paralysis sweeps over me.

And time is flying. Like a rude awakening, Natalie puts me back together again. The vulgar fluorescents are switched on. That's it then. The half hour vanishes into what seems to me to be thin air.

I open my eyes to this: Natalie's tasting me on her fingers. She's in a place that the word *heaven* doesn't

begin to describe. I could love this lovesick girl forever ... for better, for worse.

Under the Saturnian Rings I passed through the rites
of initiation into my first public orgasm. After this, public
sex will be a piece of cake.

Louise Christian

*I*t was one in the morning. In the enormous black tomb that was by day the frantic junk bond trading room, only one screen glowed green. The computer monitor on the brink of a nervous breakdown belonged to the redheaded workhorse, Louise Christian, girl millionaire.

Making her *second* million on Wall Street took far more work than she'd figured. Tonight Louise Christian worked like a dog, a mule, a beast of burden.

"Anyone making that much money deserves to work like a slave." This from her friends — sarcasm in lieu of sympathy.

Forced to suffer in silence, she wanted to throw something across the room and smash it. She was talking to herself. She was angry at herself. *Why couldn't she be content with her first million like some of her colleagues?*

And then there was her work station. It was in ruins. Crumpled papers beneath her desk spilled out of her briefcase, the receivers of the three phones were all off the hook, and her ashtray brimmed with butts.

Louise swore her computer printouts multiplied every time she turned her back on them.

She wanted to soak in a hot bath. She wanted to bake under a sun lamp. "Some 29-year-old," she said aloud, "a couple of all nighters and you turn to shit."

Louise Christian was laughing at herself. That was a good sign. But she was still talking to herself.

She searched for the light at the end of the tunnel. It was this: Tomorrow morning's quarterly meeting would be over tomorrow morning. It provided some solace. She'd have to call her girlfriend, Peach, and cancel the rendezvous she was already an hour late for. It broke her heart.

She stopped whining and dialed.

ξ

Why Kate Montgomery bothered checking the clock when the phone rang was a mystery even to her. David always called at one, one sharp, his German gene for punctuality polished to perfection.

"David, darling!" She plunged into their bedtime phone-sex ritual with a confession. "Kate was restless tonight, and, well ... she kind of started masturbating without you ... It wasn't premeditated or anything." *Little white lie.* "It just happened. You do forgive her now that she realizes how unattractive impatience can be. How lucky for me that you called in time." *Another white lie, not quite as little.* "A few minutes more and it would've all been over, and wouldn't have been half as exciting as doing it with you." *Sure, that's why she started without him.*

Silence in response to her outpouring.

"You believe me, don't you, David?"

Kate imagined him reclining in his water bed, pleased with himself, a peacock, naked, mindlessly fingering his seasick cock. She didn't want to rush him but she was halfway to orgasm. All it'd take was his voice to bring her home. If he didn't say something in *ten seconds* she was going to put him on hold and finish what she'd begun. A silent threat. Kate had no scruples when she was aroused. "You caught Kate just in time, but then we both know what good timing you have, don't we, baby?"

Nine seconds, eight seconds...

From the other end of the line a breath.

It didn't count. *Seven, six...*

Then, finally. "Good timing's my thing."

A surprisingly resonant *woman's* voice. It never occured to Kate that it might be a *stranger* calling at precisely one o'clock. She was embarrassed pink. She started giggling.

Louise was not one to pass up an opportunity pregnant with possibilities. "Personally, I think good timing is more important than good luck, don't you? Take me, for instance. Dialing the wrong number at the right time."

Louise was cool.

Kate could hear the smirk through the receiver. "You're laughing at me."

"You're right, I was ... *Kate, dear.*"

Her *name* sounded so sensual; the *dear*, so intimate. The woman's voice lingered. Eventually, Kate caught up with the conversation. "I, um, think you have the wrong number. I'm not who you expected to talk to ... I'm the wrong party."

"You want me to hang up, *Kate?*" Louise'd bet her first million that she knew the answer to that.

David could wait; Kate couldn't.

"No! Please don't! Um, I mean ... I wish you wouldn't, just yet, I mean." Hardly able to make clever conversation, Kate's feelings spilled out with a charming authenticity.

"Don't worry, *Kate,* I won't go until you want me to."

Louise switched off her computer and lamp and dumped the printouts on the carpeted floor. She kicked off her heels and swept her legs up onto her bare desk. She had license to be as dirty as she wanted to be with this turned-on, sexy stranger. *Let them try to trace this call.* She began. "Are you pretty, Kate?"

Kate didn't answer.

Louise heard a match being struck.

"You already know too much about me." Kate took in a big breath of smoke. "Tell *me* something for a change, like who are you?"

"Let's say I'm your alter ego, just for tonight."

Her alter ego. Kate liked that. "You know, you have the sexiest fucking voice."

Louise kept her sigh to herself.

"I don't believe in coincidences. You must have subconsciously wanted to dial my number," Kate said.

Would she tell David about this? It didn't have to mean she was gay. It didn't have to mean anything.

"Sounds Freudian to me, Kate. Tell me you're a shrink."

"I'm a shrink."

"A shrink in heat!"

David who?

"Caught you right smack in the middle of masturbating, did I? A dirty act, indeed, Kate."

It felt like a pilot light in her panties. Kate reddened and lowered her eyes modestly.

The hotter Kate got, the cooler Louise became. "Were you telling the truth to David or just teasing?"

"The truth."

"So you *were* halfway there when I called?"

Blush, blush, blush.

"Tell me, halfway to where?"

Listening to this female was one thing, talking to her was another. Kate got scared, had the feeling that maybe she should hang up before things got out of control. Before *things* did, or *she* did.

"Kate, if you're afraid to talk to me, then maybe I'd better go."

"—*Don't go.* You're right, I'm afraid but I'll get over it." Deep breath. "So tell me your name?"

"Louise." What the hell, she thought. "Louise Christian."

"Is that your real name?"

"Yes. My name is real, this dirty phone call is real, and talking to me is really what you want to be doing ... isn't it?" Louise wouldn't permit her to play victim tonight.

Kate was forced to lay claim to her own sexual fantasy. "You'd make a great shrink."

"You with me so far, Kate?"

If she wasn't before, Kate offered proof that she was now. "You might like to know that I'm naked from the waist down."

"That's better. So tell me what you're wearing from the waist up." Straight women never put up too big a fight.

Aroused and anxious, Kate giggled. "A tuxedo shirt ... it's my favorite. It used to be my dad's so it's gigantic on me, and the cotton's worn through. I sleep in it."

"Is it buttoned?"

"Halfway."

"Again halfway? You don't like to go all the way in anything, do you."

"Try me, Louise, I might surprise you tonight." Naturally she meant she might surprise herself.

"We'll have to see, won't we." In answer to her own rising warmth, Louise asked, "Why don't you open the rest of the buttons."

"All right."

"And describe it for me."

Kate put her cigarette in the ashtray. She swept her maize-colored bangs from her face. She was already ridiculously wet. Be brave, Kate, she told herself, before taking the plunge.

"I'm unbuttoning my shirt, Louise, one button at a time. They're tiny mother-of-pearl buttons and my nails are kind of long, so it's slow going."

Louise was in no hurry.

"My shirt's unbuttoned." She retrieved her cigarette.

"And what can you see, Kate?"

Right then Kate Montgomery knew that they were going to go all the way.

"I can see the tops of my breasts. I'm not wearing a bra tonight, Louise. I should, really, because my breasts are ... well, they're kind of—" Should she say that her breasts are large? Was that appropriate?

"Why so shy, Kate?" A shrink with a self-confidence problem, Louise saw the poetic justice in it. "I bet you're not shy watching David touch them when he makes love to you."

"I'm not quite as shy as you think." Was that a confession or an invitation, Kate wasn't sure. "You'd like my breasts."

"Would you like it if I slipped my hand inside your shirt and cupped one of them in my palm?" Louise had to lean over and switch on her small desk fan. She pointed it toward her legs.

"I love my breasts to be touched. I never get enough of that. David gets distracted, gives up too soon ... Have you been with a woman before?"

It was Louise's turn to light a cigarette. "Yes."

"I figured. You're good at this."

"So are you and you've never been with a woman."

"If you don't count that night in high school with my best friend. We'd had too much to drink."

"We don't have to count that if you don't want to. So, tell me more about your breasts."

Kate let go of her inhibitions to make room for the heat. "You'd especially like how soft they are and how white my skin is."

Louise turned up the fan speed to high. She pulled her blouse loose from her skirt. She slipped her hand beneath the black rayon to her own breast. "Are you touching them, Kate?"

"No."

"Why don't you? Slip your hand inside your father's shirt and caress your breasts, one at a time ... If it were my hands I'd feel how heavy your breasts are, cup them in the palms of my hands, and feel the weight of them." Louise began caressing her own breasts. "And while I was stroking them, Kate, I wouldn't take my eyes off your face. I'd run my fingertips around your nipples, my lips would be close to yours."

Kate hung on every word. She sat on the edge of the bed so she could see herself in the mirror.

The fan fought a losing battle trying to cool down Louise Christian. "I want you to close your eyes and feel my hand on your skin, my lips on your neck. Are you with me?"

Kate Montgomery didn't have two Ph.D.s for nothing; she'd already been touching herself. She closed her eyes and imagined. More and more she wished Louise were in the room with her. "I see you taking my breasts in your hands and lifting them to your lips."

Louise smoothly released the image: "I'm kissing Kate's nipples slowly and I can see how much she likes that. I'm licking them one at a time but so softly she can scarcely feel it—"

"—Make no mistake, Kate can feel everything."

Louise hiked her skirt up her thighs. She had on her gray silk stockings and her garter belt. She'd met Peach for a quickie at lunch. Peach loved her in garters. "Go ahead, Kate, and slip off that big old shirt."

"It's already off, sweetheart. I'm already lying on my bed naked ... waiting for you to tell me what to do for you, what to show you." Kate was going up in smoke.

Arrivederchi, David.

Why was it that the sexiest women Louise met turned out to be straight? "If I were there, Kate, I'd want to look at you. All of you, I mean. Would you get up on your knees and show it all to me?"

She watched herself in the mirror. "I'm on my knees." Kate's eagerness to please was beyond praise.

Kate imagined... *Louise behind her, stroking the backs of her thighs. She imagined Louise whispering to her that she was the most beautiful woman she'd ever been with. And she'd been with many, she said.*

"There's nothing I wouldn't show you, Louise. I'm completely open to you."

Louise hiked up her skirt higher and spread her own thighs apart. The fan was a waste of time. The heat was inside where the breeze couldn't reach. "Would you spread your legs so I could slide my fingers inside you?"

"Yes." Kate lay her cheek down on the comforter, left her ass in the air. "Go ahead and go inside me with—"

"—With what?"

"With anything you want to put inside me, Louise." *Kate was all hers.*

Kate imagined... *Louise leaning over her, her long hair tickling Kate's back. Felt Louise leaning her weight against her, wrapping her arm around her waist for support. I'm not hurting you, she heard Louise say. You couldn't, she heard herself respond. You like? Louise asked. I love! she answered. Then I want to go inside of you, Louise explained. Please do! Kate said. And Kate practically felt the woman slide her two fingers inside of her.*

Kate said, "Please put your fingers inside me."

"I am." Louise slid her fingers inside her own panties. She imagined they were Kate's.

"You'd be surprised how wet I am, Louise."

Frankly, Louise was more surprised by her own wetness. She caressed her cunt with the tips of her fingers. It was a mistake teasing herself so early on. She wouldn't hold out, she was not a patient person. You don't make a million at twenty-nine by being patient.

"I'm soaked, Louise. I wish you could feel." *When had Kate ever been this wet?* "I wish you were here to see for yourself."

It was an offer. It would be as easy as a taxicab ride.

"I wish that too, Kate, but it can't be that way tonight." Sure it could. Louise Christian was the mother of impulsivity. "Tonight we talk. That's the way it's got to be." Kate was straight. Louise Christian was protecting herself. "So, talk to me."

Kate was startled by how personally she was taking the rejection. She had more questions than answers about her behavior. To be honest, she had *no* answers, just a ground swell of feelings. "I'm still on all fours, but I have my hand on my cunt and I am stroking myself, Louise. That's what you want, isn't it?"

"It's exactly what I want." Louise pulled off her panties and dropped them in the top drawer of her desk. Then she reported it. "I just took off my panties because I want to feel how wet you've made me and I want to tell you all about it." She kept her thighs together and slid her hand between them and touched her pussy. And sighed, "Kate, Kate..." *For crying out loud, why'd she have to be straight?*

"Talk to me, Louise, please, tell me what you feel, where you are, what you're wearing."

"I'm at my office on Wall Street and it's deserted. Just me and one hundred and twelve empty desks. I'm turning on my lamp. It's dim but I can see. I'm wearing a black blouse and a tight burgundy linen skirt. And I'm wearing hose and garters. You wouldn't be able to stop yourself from running your hand up my thighs if you were here. My legs are braced against the edge of my desk and I've pushed my skirt up to my hips. I can't see my cunt but I can see my red triangle of hair."

A sleeping fire awakened in Kate.

This was the redhead's forte: starting fires in women and then extinguishing them.

Kate shut her eyes. "If you were here with me now I'd want you to touch every inch of me."

"And you know I have gentle hands."

"Then run them through my hair. And I'll open my legs for you as wide as you want. I'll lift up my hips so you can put your face on me, your mouth on my clit. I wouldn't be able to lay still, I know I wouldn't."

Considering Louise's weak willpower when it came to women, she was holding her own remarkably well. She'd either come or combust. "Spread your lips apart for me." She was getting wetter with each word. That was the idea. "I want to slide my fingers inside you."

Kate vibrated with the woman's voice. She was hotter than hell. "Do it, Louise, I'm holding my lips apart, I want you in. I'm dripping wet. Why won't you come and push me over the edge. Don't make me do it myself."

What was she saying? Kate didn't know, she didn't care. She was floating in a swirling current of feelings, propelled into the provocative unknown. "I want you to see me, touch me. My ass is in the air waiting for your mouth." She felt her heart beating hard. "I can't wait much longer." Really hard. "I've got to come."

"Then do it, Kate, do it with me. I have my hand on my pussy and I'm trying to go slowly but I can't." Louise's spirit was willing to wait, her flesh wasn't. Her body resented the slow hands. Everything inside her told her to go, to move, to fly.

Louise Christian's sexuality was a vital force in her life. Women either moved with it or moved out of its way.

Kate let the steamroller in.

"Close your eyes, Kate, and think of my hands and my fingers and my three gold rings on each pinky ... Imagine me caressing your clit, stroking your lips, teasing your pussy ... But not going inside you ... yet."

The receiver was held firmly in place between Louise's ear and her shoulder. Her hands were free. They moved urgently between her shaved lips. They insisted.

"You're going to grab my wrists, Kate, and push my hand down on your cunt. You're going to want it harder because I'm just barely touching your lips ... barely touching your skin ... barely stroking the hairs on your pussy so that it's tickling you and making you greedy for more ... Much more."

Louise's fingers moved demandingly over her clit. She was doing to herself what she said she wouldn't do to Kate. And Kate was doing the same thing rubbing her palm against her clitoris. Both women on the ascent, both after the same brass ring, both not doing a goddamned thing they were told.

"You can feel my fingers near your vagina but they're not near enough, and Kate, you can feel my fingers down by your asshole but they're not near enough."

Kate's heart pounded in fits and starts. Her abdominal muscles were hard, her shoulders tense, her legs rigid. Her focus fixed on one point in time: the point when her body would collide with the orgasm now en route. And submit to it. Kate could see it coming. Her body was primed for its arrival. Come covered her cunt. The orgasm was going to be upon her in no time.

Louise beat her to it. The sensation spread up her calves, her knees, the insides of her thighs until it compressed in her cunt and detonated in a flash. Louise raised her hand to her mouth.

Kate heard her muffle the groan. Kate was perfect stillness, listening. She imagined being next to her: holding Louise while her body stirred with the orgasm, running her hands through the woman's hair, kissing her damp brow, her eyelids, her everything.

Feelings flashed full blast — receiver to receiver, Wall Street to Riverside Drive.

"My turn," Kate announced.

"Yes, baby, it's your turn."

"I have my hands all over my pussy. You take my hand and lick each of my fingers. You taste my sugar." Kate brought her fingers to her mouth and licked the warm liquid.

Tenderly, "Go on." Louise's heart had once been broken by a straight woman. But she survived. Louise should be going to this wild woman, racing to her, flying to her side. "Go on."

"You slip my clit between your lips ... and you're going to suck me ... and you're not going to stop until I come in your mouth." Kate had to hold on to the headboard with her free hand. Her legs were trembling so badly they could no longer be trusted for support. She stroked her cunt; her need was sharp, her hands moved swiftly over the cherry-red thing. A pearl-white come coated her fingers. It was important that she not stop. Her lips were in full, swollen, overripe bloom. Kate threw her head back with the orgasm and cried out.

Louise closed her eyes and took it in. She felt it in her own body. Saw it all in front of her. To be near Kate now, on top of her, holding her down, restraining her unruly body—

—Kate cried out Louise's name. A flawless orgasm rang through her body. Her hair and feelings tumbled freely everywhere. Her cunt was on fire. Hot lava on her fingers burned her skin but her hands wouldn't let go. She didn't want the seduction to end; it was just beginning, damn it. To Louise it might be just coincidental anonymous sex. But to her it was like being resuscitated, given mouth-to-mouth with pure electricity, at once perilous and passionate. The puzzle of Kate Montgomery's life dropped on the floor and scattered into a thousand pieces. Nothing fit anymore. She said it point blank: 5900 Riverside Drive, Apartment 6E.

Louise's taxicab got her there in twenty minutes.

Virginia Reardon

*V*irginia Reardon hit the JFK terminal and knew she was wet without even touching herself. It didn't take a genius to figure it out. The unwelcoming sterile airport, the crowds of particularly pushy tourists, and the long wait for her luggage did nothing to dissipate her desire. All around her in the cavernous baggage claim area were children yelping and parents scolding and bellcaps shouting, and Virginia's mounting desire mounting.

The company limousine pulled up twenty minutes late. The driver was an art student; she'd been late to every appointment every day of her life. She bolted madly from the car, the *fuck* word coursing through her veins. *"Weekend traffic,"* she said. It was a plea to the black woman who awaited her. She was the first girl driver hired in this uptight company, the test case. She opened the door for the vice president of affiliate sales, her eyes pleading with her not to lodge a complaint.

Virginia could feel the girl sweat. Nobody should have to beg. "Relax," she said, "it happens."

The girl helped her into the limo. She closed the door with great care. She heaved a man-sized sigh, she needed the job, she wanted the money. Art supplies were murder on her cash flow.

Inside the car, Virginia could smell new leather. She got comfortable. The air conditioning felt cool and Virginia was getting hotter. She slipped down into the cushioned red leather seat.

Without warning, a seamless cascade of dirty images filled Virginia's imagination. Virginia was helpless to suppress them, helpless not to respond. Perhaps it was because her period was due any minute, or her girlfriend was away in the Grand Canyon backpacking, or because she'd just closed a critical sale. Or was it her red satin panties ... Who knew?

Who cared?

Virginia struggled in earnest to keep her hands from her lap, but her arousal was already out of hand.

In front, the young chauffeur with the untamed, short blonde hair exited JFK en route to Virginia's Soho loft. She ran her hands through her hair twice; she'd never seen a more beautiful woman.

Privacy was miles and miles out of Virginia's reach. She didn't want to tell the girl to rush because the girl seemed nervous enough. But gravity pulled the Reardon hands down, down, down. It was simple physics, really. Her fresh damp rude cunt was like a magnet, impossible to resist, and yet Virginia was determined to fight the good fight. She withdrew the annual report from her briefcase, cemented her long ebony fingers to the sales figures, and studied, or pretended to, and dared defy her most primitive urge.

Apparently it was business as usual for the driver, as if a bloody primal battle of wills was not being fought in the backseat. Clearly, the white girl was not paying attention.

Hardly. But she was forcing herself to keep her eyes on the road.

Within the not-too-safe sanctuary of Virginia's imagination, images taunted her ... her smoky musk scent, her cocoa lips buried beneath red panties ... warm cream between warm thighs. *All-too-realistic images.* Virginia Reardon's need was great. But it was overshadowed by the girl three feet in front of her. Surely the girl would know. Yet her knowing would make it all the more thrilling. If celibate success was measured in minutes, two reassuring ones had passed without incident. But still, relentless urges urged Virginia to do the terribly private thing in this terribly public place.

And the more she thought of the blonde seeing everything, the more she knew she had to wait. And the more excited she got. Only the girl stood between her and her need. Virginia threw a challenging look at her in the rearview mirror. Blue eyes versus brown, girl versus woman and the thin ice beneath the Reardon willpower thinned...

ξ

The victory of nature over willpower was marked with a single magnificent smile. *Virginia's.*

It was obviously time. Time to bring her imagination to fruition. Time to do it but not let the girl see it — that was her compromise with her conscience.

The sales figures disappeared into the black hole of her briefcase. Virginia's fingers moved like secrets between the folds of her floor-length alpaca overcoat to her trousers. Beneath mocha fingers the zipper gave way like butter, like the parting of the Red Sea. Virginia lifted herself off the seat enough to slide her slacks down beneath her hips, then her ass. She flirted with the idea of sliding her pants down around her ankles, but she was daring, not delinquent. Her pants stayed put.

The deceptively innocent-looking driver sensed something. She exchanged a serious look with the pretty passenger in her rearview, unbuttoned her collar, and made a benign comment about the weather.

Then came Virginia Reardon's first touch of flesh. A kiss of a touch that hardly called attention to itself. She spread apart the tops of her oven-warm thighs. What would her girlfriend think of her now, Virginia wondered — bank manager Jane, conservative Jane. *Jane would kill her.* Virginia concentrated instead on the girl half her age in the front seat who could almost reach out and touch her if she wanted to. Virginia slid down in her leather seat to allow her fingers room. They swept along the tenderest, smoothest flesh closest to her cunt. With each brush stroke of her clever fingers, her thumb or palm *accidently* brushed against the panel of her panties — a damp panel that held hostage the burnt-almond lips of her pussy.

The driver's blue eyes brimmed with question marks. Inexplicably restless, the girl shifted in her seat, her hair no longer the only unrestrained thing. She lit a Marlboro, turned on the radio, and told Virginia they were halfway to Soho.

Brown eyes smiled as Reardon fingers pushed aside the elastic of her panties. Quick as a wish her fingertips were on the lips of her pussy. Delighted fingers caressed short hairs sticky with cream. Sienna-colored lips slick with gloss and heating up. Virginia's tickling fingers caused the sweetest stirrings. On slow wings her fingers traced a trail of come across the length of her lips as far down as she could reach. All the way down to the pursed little rigid mouth of her ass. Austere lips always receptive to the touch of liquid fingertips. The stern little thing gave way with just the touch of the salty mother-of-pearl milk.

The New York City skyline, as striking as it was at dusk, blurred beneath Virginia's suddenly heavy-lidded bedroom eyes.

Through the plume of smoke she exhaled, the driver divided her time unevenly between the road and the rearview mirror. She explained that this was a part-time job to support her passion for art; she had a year left at Parsons School of Design. Then she became silent again.

The blonde's voice was a turn-on. Virginia's eyes were glued to the girl, and her cream-coated fingertips were glued to her own pussy. She explored the loose moist folds that thickened under the playful scratchings of her long nails. She eased two fingers between her sticky lips. The small pulsing between her legs tugged at the sensitive walls of her vagina, it would not be ignored. Virginia heeded its call. Her fingers closed in on her clit, the clit that made glorious things happen in her body.

The woman was black magic to the girl. The girl tensed her ass, shifted in her seat for the fiftieth time, and nailed her fists to the steering wheel. That she fucking couldn't turn around was torture. That she couldn't actually see a damn thing in the mirror wasn't the point.

Virginia didn't want to come like a madwoman. She had in mind an orgasm more like a lullaby or a sweet nothing. After all, she didn't want the girl to know.

Of course she wanted her to know.

Virginia's eyes locked with the girl's as the bold fingers of her left hand spread apart her yielding lips. Fingers, bolder still, rubbed up against the sides of her teardrop clit like a kitty. Languidly, Virginia's unswerving fingertips massaged. Colors clashed: red nail polish against redder clit.

—Not a single thought of Jane resurfaced, no trace of her anywhere—

The driver shoved a hand in her front pocket and went after her lighter, again. A thinly veiled excuse to brush her hand against her own cunt. She couldn't prove anything, but she *knew* that look in the black woman's eyes and that unmistakable distant scent that a female never forgets. She was only twenty, but already she knew about these things. If she was wet, she wouldn't be surprised.

Virginia's fingers were lenient with a cunt so *seemingly* slow to respond. She patiently caressed the tips of the curly hairs around her clitoris. Arousal mounted not-too-privately between Virginia's tense thighs. She kept from closing her eyes. High heels dug down into the thick taupe carpet. Virginia's hands moved imperceptibly beneath her coat. Her fingertips held her swollen lips apart, giving her entree into her vagina. She took advantage of it. She stroked her swollen clitoris. Dipped and stroked, stroked and dipped.

...It was so subtle, in fact, that Virginia Reardon stirred with the orgasm rather than shaking with it. She was lulled into the climax rather than lurched. She sighed with the coming rather than shouting. Virginia kept her eyes fixed on the driver and let the girl watch her come.

There was no way the girl could have missed it. The irregular breathing, the moist brow. The tropical scent alone.

When the car pulled over at the corner of Spring and Wooster, the blonde raced to open the door for the vice president. The girl, too, was out of breath. The girl was blushing.

Virginia couldn't help but smile. She slipped a twenty into the girl's palm with lingering fingers still slicked. As a bonus Virginia Reardon left behind her scent, her flavor, and an unmistakable creamy trace of come.

The girl never took tips. This one she took.

Grace & Sonia

Sonia wasn't new to girl bars. Still she hated them. Summer heat in the form of a pale blonde in a red sundress at the far end of the bar was troubling her. Sonia swept her bangs from her eyes and stared and stared and drank and drank. Desire was drumming in the chest of Sonia Precci beneath her ample breasts.

And the pale blonde could almost hear it from across the dark, narrow, noisy room.

Sonia wrestled with the king-sized schoolgirl crush. But Sonia was no schoolgirl; schoolgirls didn't sit in a Greenwich Village girl bar on a school night looking to find themselves in a woman.

And it was no one-way worship either — Grace Shepherd was attracted right back. Grace had had her fill of touching without tenderness and flirting without friendship. The stranger looked bright, clever, fun. She reeked of potential.

This was Sonia's first time in a bar since Frances left her for a man eight months ago. Sonia'd been a fool for the female for six years. Tonight she wanted a woman to make her forget Frances. She wanted Frances back. Sonia stared and stared.

Grace stood up. Her lips turned to parchment, her resolve dissolved, and she swallowed hard and sat back down. Grace was hardly the shy attorney in a courtroom. But Grace was not good at opening lines with women. Really, not good.

Sonia caught a flash of red high heels and the female's perfectly bare, perfectly white legs. She'd have to take the blonde to the beach to tan her. To touch her.

It was a provocative twenty-minute staredown.

It was feeding time for Sonia Precci. She grabbed her clutch bag from the bar.

Long legs made long strides toward her. Grace licked her lips, tasted the possibilities. Grace took in the beauty ... the softly square face, the wavy chestnut-colored hair. The female's soulful brown eyes, however, were too much to bear.

Hindsight told Sonia that she should've stopped after her first martini, intuition told her that she was already wet. She slipped into the seat beside Grace.

Grace prepared to be sucked right up into the woman.

Sonia ran a fingertip along Grace's wrist and re-marked, "You're so blonde!"

The touch was sweet, it tickled. Grace laughed and said, "Yes."

Sonia asked, "Are you gay?"

"Yes again."

"Are you sure?"

Easy laughter. Grace nodded.

Sonia wanted to know if Grace wanted to talk.

For the third time Grace said, "Yes." When was the last time a woman asked her to talk, just talk. Grace got her hopes up.

"Because if I'm not mistaken," Sonia said, "isn't something supposed to come before the sex part?"

So it *was* going to be a physical thing tonight. No big surprise. Success took priority and relationships took time and something swift and anonymous was all Grace left time for. Besides, Grace's married girlfriends always said that anonymous sex was hottest.

Grace threw Sonia a stupendous open-mouth smile. "Foreplay comes before the sex part and this conversation hardly rates as foreplay."

Sonia paid for both drinks and tipped extravagantly. The bartender was a pretty girl ... and one never knew.

"It feels like foreplay to me and I should know," Sonia quipped, "because I'm a doctor and doctors know everything."

Grace disagreed. "It's lawyers that know everything." *A doctor!* Her imagination crossed the boundaries of moderation and good taste. She, too, stood. She pulled Sonia so close that her breath escaped into Sonia's mouth. Then Grace changed her mind and took a step back and perused.

The good doctor was a slave to this kind of thing. She was the examiner, never the examined. For her, being looked at was hotter than being touched, hotter than being undressed. Small rapid breaths were the first clue. Then there was the buzz between her legs. Her cheeks and throat reddened. Warm, she felt very warm. She closed her eyes and felt the body, then the breath, then the lips, then the kiss. Heat filled her mouth.

Their lipstick was history. So was the bar. The two made an in-office appointment for six the next night.

For as far back as Grace Shepherd could remember, love had been her oldest fantasy. Playing doctor was the second oldest.

ξ

Altruistic hands explored Grace's body. Wise hands softened her defenses. Agile hands erased her tension. Attentive hands relaxed her as she was touched everywhere by the healing hands. She lay quietly on the leather examination table and trusted. Grace tried to be accommodating for, after all, she was the patient.

Fingertips feigning neutrality gently probed. The doctor in the white lab coat sensed stress. "I promise not to bite," she said, much as she wanted to. It was a fine line. Sonia practiced restraint for, after all, she was the doctor.

Educated hands swept over Grace's gown, untied it, spread it apart. Sonia had made her get into that starched white thing and lie down on the cold exam table and wait.

There no longer was any question of who was in charge.

Grace waited twenty minutes before Sonia re-entered the room.

The doctor explained slowly, "I need you to be as relaxed as possible. It's easier to distinguish things that way."

Coyly, "What things … Doctor?" As if Grace didn't know.

"Things like your natural reflexes," Sonia replied. *Things like your soft breasts* was what she meant.

"Things like tender spots near joints or any pressure zones," Sonia added. *The sweet curve of your fanny and all zones erotic* was what she meant.

The doctor couldn't help herself for, after all, she was only human.

God knows they both wanted to do the same thing right there on the leather exam table. But that was out of the question…

So soon, that is.

The patient felt heat emanating from the hands on her abdomen. Grace concentrated on those hands: the wide palms, long fingers, short practical nails with clear polish, the miniature medical class ring on the pinky of her right hand.

Sonia's fingers simmered with desire.

Grace felt the hurry in the hands and said so.

Take your time, there *is* no fire, Sonia told herself. She went to the window, slowed herself down, then returned to the patient. Her curious hands in search of glands mounted the 33-year-old body.

Healing hands, sublime body.

Here, where most patients demurely averted their eyes, this adventuress kept hers steady on the doctor. Grace raised her arms without timidity. She watched the healer dispatch benevolent fingertips in search of glandular swellings. *Misguided fingertips,* she thought.

"You're searching for swellings in all the wrong places, Doctor."

"I met you in a wrong place, Grace."

"Wrong for all the right reasons."

"Miss Shepherd, you're distracting me."

"I should hope so."

Sonia probed the patient's underarms. She was precise in measuring the pressure against the gentleness of her touch. She was expert at it.

Sonia had not asked Grace to lower her arms and Grace did not volunteer. Grace felt unnaturally open. But beneath her slick, corporate veneer, openness was Grace's natural state. She'd simply forgotten that.

After a delicate surveillance, the doctor declared that all of Grace's glands were as nature had intended.

"God's been generous," Grace smiled.

Sonia gave Grace the once-over and said, "I'd say She's been most generous."

Sonia pulled out the black-and-chrome stethoscope. "You're going to like this."

"No more than you will."

"The metal might feel cold against your skin," Sonia warned.

"I'll be brave."

"That's a good girl," Sonia said, then laid the cold instrument against Grace's flesh.

And brave or not, Grace flinched.

The doctor smiled, listened, and looked in silence.

"What do you hear?" Grace asked.

"Life!" Sonia said.

"What does 'Life!' sound like?"

Unable to explain it, Sonia put the stethoscope to her own chest and let Grace listen.

"I don't hear anything," Grace lied.

So the doctor undid the top button of her lab coat and the top two buttons of her silk blouse. She placed the instrument against the bare flesh of her breast.

"Ah ... that's better," Grace exclaimed.

"You're telling me, Miss Shepherd." Sonia stood still a while as her heart beat hard and her patient listened with closed eyes.

And the already blurred doctor–patient boundary blurred further.

Dr. Precci moved on and it was not a question of timing, but rather how long she'd be able to hold out.

She put her hands on the patient's neck. It was such a lovely neck, exquisite like a ballerina's, and she wanted to kiss it. Sonia held it between her hands and watched Grace lean her head back. A subtle yielding.

—And how could Sonia not remember that gesture? Frances dropped her head back like that when she gave into an orgasm—

"Have you examined your breasts lately?" Sonia asked.

"No," Grace answered, having examined them only the day before.

Sonia said, "Then I'll have to do it for you."

She'd have to, as if she wasn't dying to.

Dr. Precci rested her palms upon the patient's breasts, then closed her eyes.

Grace sighed and closed her eyes, too.

A professional examination of Grace's breasts would be a test for them both. *A bitch of a test.*

Calmly, "Now Grace, don't be alarmed if this part of the exam arouses you."

"You mean, you'd be disappointed if it didn't!"

"What makes you think you know what I mean?"

"*Dirty girls are my specialty*," Grace said. "And what's yours, Doctor?"

"Examining them."

That was it! Sonia leaned over Grace to kiss those gorgeous lips that she'd been coveting. Her subconcious said *go*, her conscious said *no*, and Sonia, a Libra, couldn't decide. So she went back to work.

Each Shepherd breast was cupped beneath a caressing Precci palm. Hands engulfed and squeezed the C-cup breasts with a poignant pressure. Abundant, plentiful, white-on-white breasts.

And despite extensive efforts at emotional neutrality, Dr. Precci's medicinal ministrations had "sensual" written all over them. *Detachment was impossible.* There was love in Sonia's touch despite herself. Frances had wounded her, not killed her.

And fondled by the learned hands, the patient was having no easy time of it herself.

So it was no wonder that by the time the doctor's fingertips grazed the patient's primrose nipples they were hard.

"Perhaps we'd better stop examining your breasts," the wise doctor suggested.

"Oh my, and you warned me this might happen!" Some coquettish blushing and flushing followed.

Sonia helped Grace sit up and move to the end of the table. Her legs dangled over the edge. It was chilly in the exam room and Grace's hands and feet were cold.

Grace didn't notice but Sonia did. She took the woman's hands in her own and rubbed them. She blew a long, kind, warm breath on them.

Such true affection did not go unnoticed by either woman.

The doctor explained, "This is where—"

Grace couldn't wait!

"—I test your reflexes."

Naturally, it was a letdown.

The doctor tested one knee, then the other. Then she examined Grace's thighs, calves, ankles, feet, toes.

After an exhilarating exploration, the doctor said, "Everything looks ... wonderful."

One had only to look at Grace for proof of that.

"Should I take off my gown, Dr. Precci?"

"Please leave those decisions to me." Then she spread Grace's legs apart and looked at her with that I-don't-believe-I'll-ever-get-enough-of-you look.

Nothing about Grace Shepherd was timid, but Grace bit down on her lower lip, faking timidity anyway.

The doctor asked if this graphic examination made her uncomfortable.

Grace admitted that maybe it did, slightly.

Oh, please!

"That's too bad." Of course, the doctor understood.

"How can I trust that this is really part of a routine physical?" The patient angled for the truth. She had a right to know.

"I can't help you until you trust me, Grace. Trust," she said suggestively, "is everything." Then Sonia spread the patient's thighs apart even farther.

Sonia reached for the halogen swinging lamp above the exam table and pulled it toward Grace.

Grace's heart squealed with delight.

"It's best that there's nothing hidden between doctor and patient," Sonia said, turning on the high beam. "I can't help you if you don't show me everything."

"Everything, Doctor?!" Grace whispered, working herself up into a sweet little frenzy.

"Everything."

Perfect. Grace sighed her consent.

Sonia instructed Grace to lie back.

Sonia lifted a metal instrument from the side table. "I'll be sliding this inside your vagina."

Grace was all ears.

"And it might not feel entirely pleasant."

"Are you going to hurt me, Dr. Precci?"

"I'll do my best."

Sonia washed her hands, dried them, and stretched a pair of thin rubber gloves over them. Sonia pulled the high beam above Grace's pelvis. "Lie still now, so that I can have an unobstructed view."

Grace did as she was told but it was no small challenge.

"Shamans can tell the severity of an illness by the scent of a patient," Sonia explained. She lowered her head only inches from Grace's flesh and subtly inhaled what should have been the fragrance of the female.

Grace disliked smells. Sonia lived for them.

How Sonia wished Grace hadn't showered tonight. Scents were so important to her that to smell no trace of female bewildered her. The Sicilian physician went out in search of the scent. There was a temper in her rough touch, in the way she set aside the metal instrument, in the way she took the gown off Grace and told her to turn over onto her stomach.

Facedown, Grace could see nothing but could feel everything. She felt a purring at the base of her throat. It was all she could do to keep still. The hands returned to her shoulders but the touch did not calm her. The anxious hands made her want to drag the doctor's body down on her own.

A primitive chord resonated between them.

Sonia swung the high beam directly above the patient's ass. Nothing could possibly remain secret in such a light. Sonia took the firm, round cheeks in hand and parted them.

Grace was not breathing.

Here, Sonia thought, the scent of the female, shower or no, was not to be erased. An earthy scent, authentic, untampered with. It stirred her. It made further delay painful. Sonia parted Grace's legs slowly.

There were nail marks in Grace's palms. "Must you go so slowly?"

"In a doctor's office, the doctor's in charge," Sonia reminded her.

"This patient's not into delayed gratification."

"I know, Miss Shepherd, now lie still!"

With two seductive snaps, the rubber gloves were gone. Sonia spilled warm oil in the palms of her hands and began fingering Grace.

Grace shut her eyes, sighed twice.

Sonia spent time investigating the tightness of one hole and the looseness of the other. She didn't enter either. "Do you feel my fingers, Grace?"

They were all Grace *could* feel.

"Do they make you nervous?"

It was an exhale more than a no, but it was a no.

"That's a good sign."

"Of?"

"Of things to come, Grace, of course." Sonia left it at that.

Oil spilled onto the base of Grace's back. Sonia bent her head and dropped kisses two inches apart across Grace's shoulders ... down Grace's spine ... up the curve of her ass ... down Grace's slender thighs and backs of her knees. The cascade of kisses came to an end when Sonia reached Grace's toes.

The patient was dubious. "Dr. Precci, so you're sure that this is part of a *normal* physical?"

"Who's to say what's normal, Miss Shepherd?"

And one by one Sonia slipped each toe into her mouth, running her tongue against the soft skin between them, careful to arouse, not tickle. She nipped at them, sucked on them. From the biggest to the babe, each was licked wet, soaked and sucked on, kissed and caressed. When Sonia was done, she slid her mouth over the soles of Grace's feet. She took the slender ankles into her mouth, bit down softly into her raised arches, then changed directions and headed north.

Grace was suffering. The delay was misery. Exhilarating, resuscitating, mouth-watering misery.

Sonia's sweetheart lips moved back upstream to Grace's shapely calves, to the perfumed-scented backs of her knees, then to the thighs expectant beneath her palms, and finally to the patient's ass where the kissing came to an end.

Sonia retrieved four velvet-covered bindings from the drawer labelled *Sterile*.

She'd thought it a dozen times. "You are a thing of beauty, Grace Shepherd."

She fastened Grace's legs to the metal stirrups. She lifted Grace's arms above her head and secured them as well.

Grace was forced to lie facedown, bound and vulnerable.

The doctor's strong oiled hands spread themselves across the unblemished skin of Grace's back, pressing her into further submission, if further submission was possible.

Grace tested her wrist restraints. Her arms had that faraway ache she knew from experience would only worsen. She moaned low when she felt warm oil dripping down the crease of her fanny, felt fingertips rubbing up against her asshole, felt the cold steel.

"Penetration makes me crazy," Grace whispered.

Sonia's chest tightened with anticipation.

Grace stiffened as the cool heat eased into her from behind. The heavy silver thing in Sonia's palm slid in smoothly, the steel cooled her insides.

Grace had never been this intimate, never let anyone or anything inside her bottom before. Her mind went blank, she would let Sonia do her thinking for her now.

Grace instinctively arched back. The fullness of it was pleasurably painful. Had her arms and legs been free, she would've gotten up on all fours. Grace lifted her backside off the table. She wasn't surprised to hear herself panting. Tight and full, she wanted it badly and she hoped Sonia could see that.

Sonia could see that and more. Under the halogen, the cream between Grace's thighs glistened — cream that soon would be smeared across the grainy leather beneath Grace's body.

Grace would've brought herself to orgasm with the silver thing if it were up to her. She wanted Sonia to hold her down and fuck her. She *could* take it in, she knew she could.

It'd be months before Sonia would learn that she could easily outdistance Grace, that Grace always threw in the towel early.

Still in her white lab coat, Sonia made her move. She climbed up on the table and sat astride the woman. She slid the silver bolt inside Grace one final time. She slipped her other hand to Grace's pussy. Brilliant red lips dripped a wet welcome for her.

How much Sonia needed that kind of a reception from a woman. How deeply Frances had hurt her.

Grace felt the fingers on her clitoris.

Sonia felt the murmur of orgasm in Grace's womb. She laid her full weight down on Grace.

Grace strained to get to her knees and push the vibrator further into her ass.

"Lie still, Grace, lie still," Sonia urged.

As if Grace could. Grace was moaning. Grace was coming. Grace was tied down. Her wrists hurt, her ankles hurt, and the velvet knots did not loosen even one merciful inch.

Grace's soft spots were vincible and under siege and yet, in her gut, Grace trusted Sonia not to hurt her. She was sure Sonia wasn't the hurting kind.

Grace rubbed her belly and breasts against the wet leather. She slid her body back and forth in time with Sonia's. Her blonde hair fell into her eyes and she could not see. And she *could not* lie still. And her delicate and slippery clit was coming and going. *The wildcat wanted freedom, she didn't want to come in captivity.*

Sonia loved this, she fucking loved this.

Grace wrestled with the velvet restraints to no avail, for it was quicksand, this orgasm, and it dragged her down despite herself. Grace surrendered to it, threw her head back.

Instantly, Sonia recognized that gesture. It would be a long time before she'd think of Frances again.

Grace's cunt released the stunning scent and rich cream that jarred Sonia back into the moment.

Feelings fresh and new and unexpected surfaced. Feelings impossible to name slithered into the slight space between the sweating bodies of the two females.

The feelings, the tears, the scent, the sweat, the come had the makings of one messy and gorgeous affair.

Vanessa & Betty

Redheads were Betty's favorites. Curly red pubes and see-through skin and nasty tempers. This redhead brought out the worst in her. This one, half her size, was looking for a fight. The girl's belligerence turned Betty right the fuck on. She snapped her fingers for a barmaid. The studs on her leather wristband sparkled by candlelight.

Vanessa Noble ran her fingertips along Betty's matching choker and let loose a chilling smile. She'd never been more drunk in her young life.

Betty was going to make this lush tonight.

The Noble girl wanted Betty from the first, all five-feet-ten of her busty body. Frightening and forbidding, Betty excited the hell out of her.

Mid-conversation in the corner of the dive that passed for a lesbian leather bar, Betty offered her name.

Vanessa cut her off before she got into any bad habits.

Betty had had few illusions when the redhead first put the moves on her; now she had none. "You don't want to know my name?"

"Really not interested in girl talk."

With the back of her hand Betty could wipe the cocky smile from the girl's blue eyes, teach her a thing or two.

"I'd have asked if I wanted to know." Vanessa couldn't get enough of big girls like Betty; their threatening looks thrilled her.

Vanessa was no match for Betty. They both knew that.

Not here, not yet, Betty told herself. "No names. Then I guess I call you Red and you call me Lady X."

"Lady X! Perfect." Vanessa laughed aloud. "This round's on me. Tomorrow I'm off to Manhattan so tonight I'm celebrating."

"What have you got against Boston?"

"There's nothing here for me."

"Something as pretty as you doesn't have a girlfriend hidden somewhere?" God knows Betty had four.

"I did, but I don't like strings, so I broke it off last night."

"Broke it off just like that!"

Vanessa echoed, "Just like that." Not really just like that.

Betty said she ended affairs with flowers, candy.

Vanessa loved it, a leather bruiser with a lamb's heart. "Shit happens, Lady X. She'll live."

"Were you at least nice to her when you did it?" The sassy bitch had no feelings.

"I'm not a nice girl, I don't do nice things. Can't you tell?" Big talk, big heat.

"That's why you've come to me, Red."

Juices were flowing.

Laughter came from the redhead who burned and pillaged everyone in her wake, or, at least, wanted Betty to think so.

Betty wasn't fooled. Let the girl pretend all she wanted, Betty had had enough talk for one night. "C'mon with me, Red, I got a treat in store for you."

It wouldn't be long now before Vanessa got what was coming to her. She couldn't wait.

Neither could Betty. Betty helped Vanessa to her feet, put her on the back of her cycle and beat a one-way, back-road path for the motel in Lynn where she took all her girls.

Tearing up the asphalt underneath the tires, spitting up gravel and dusty dirt, the Harley literally flew down the fucking road.

Betty was speeding like a maniac, splitting open with the energy. She had plans for Vanessa.

The wind was wild at seventy-five miles per hour. Vanessa's eyes stung, her perm was a lost cause.

"Shit!" Betty squealed at the yellow light and accelerated. The hot rubber smells from her tires excited her.

Cars whizzed by — nothing more than shots of color and light in this foreplay that was working the redhead into a frenzy.

Betty wanted to drive right through the motel front door like this — piss the pussycat off so she could watch the wavy curly frizzy red mane of hair go up in flames.

The speedometer climbed to eighty, eighty-five, ninety. The Noble girl loved the speed, the danger, loved it on the edge where she felt most alive.

Betty made a death-defying left turn from the right-hand lane. She swept around a series of blocks and came to a screeching halt in front of the motel.

Vanessa swung open the door of the motel room.

Lynn, Massachusetts, at two in the morning was no time to be choosy.

Besides, Vanessa had come for one thing only. Even kissing was beside the point.

She led Betty to the bed, unbuttoned the dyke's stiff black vest.

Betty leaned back against the headboard, entrusted herself to the kid.

They hadn't done a damn thing yet, but Vanessa was having a great fucking time. She dragged the vest off the woman and whipped open the snaps on the denim work shirt. She threw the shirt on the floor.

Betty prepared for the ultimate unveiling.

Vanessa unfastened the bra and laid her eyes on the leather dyke's queen-sized breasts.

Betty was mighty proud of those breasts. They rendered the girls speechless. And Vanessa was no exception. Betty watched the girl's appetite enlarge.

Vanessa buried her face in the mounds of flesh.

Betty embraced the girl with her strong arms and rocked the redhead as she might a child. Her maternal instincts surfaced. She knew the difference between a girl wanting to be fucked and needing to be held.

Enfolded in the bigness of Betty, Vanessa nestled in. The bear hug was pure affection, very endearing.

Betty made nice. "Come to big Momma, baby girl."

If Vanessa wanted nice she would've still been with her lover. *She remembered what she'd come for.* She incited the dyke. "Can't you just fuck a girl without talking!"

Betty grabbed the little bitch who'd jerked her off one too many times and held her down and stripped her.

Vanessa protested the excessive use of force. But she loved every minute of it.

Every time Betty warmed toward the girl, the bitch turned on her. Obviously the girl wanted her fun rougher. Betty obliged.

Vanessa wrestled to top the dyke who was twice her size with twice the strength.

Vanessa's laughter provoked Betty. The girl was half her age — assuming the bobby-soxer was even eighteen — and Betty didn't want trouble. She let the girl top her.

Vanessa pinned Betty down on her back, straddled her, dug her knees into Betty's arms.

Betty had to laugh.

The dyke was laughing at her. Vanessa bore down harder.

It didn't take much for Betty to flip the girl over.

Vanessa cried out; Lord, she loved it.

Betty put her hand to the girl's mouth. "No talking, remember!" It pleased her to have the last word with the naked girl writhing beneath her thick forearms.

To Vanessa, fighting and fucking were all the same.

With her hand glued to Vanessa's mouth, Betty warned the girl not to make a sound.

Vanessa's blue, blue eyes sparkled. She promised.

Betty stood up. She pulled off her black boots, her skin-tight leather pants, then her underwear and socks.

Vanessa broke her promise. *"Do anything you want to me."*

Betty had every intention of doing just that.

"Don't stop no matter what, okay?" The redhead was begging for trouble. She got up on all fours. Vanessa was deliciously nervous.

Betty got on the bed with the volatile female. She'd fuck the redhead when *she* was good and ready. Betty took her by the shoulders and she was not gentle.

Neither was Vanessa.

Betty turned the girl around, grabbed a fistful of red hair, and pulled it back. Then she kissed her. Betty thrust her tongue practically down the throat of the girl who made her hot, made her angry, made her want to fuck her until she cried *uncle.*

Vanessa let the tongue drive into her.

Betty would show her who was boss.

Vanessa never wanted the role. She responded to Betty's every move. She tongued the woman back. Vanessa was lost in the deep-throat kiss, her mouth engulfed by the dyke's. She wanted the hands that pulled her hair to pull harder. Her mouth was open, her throat exposed.

Betty's tongue pumped into the girl, penetrated her like her fingers soon would.

Vanessa pulled free. Her lips sought out the large brown nipples.

Betty's breasts were the most sensitive part of her body. She made it easy for Vanessa, she lifted her breasts to the girl's mouth.

It was a tender act. A sober look passed between the women, who knew exactly what they were doing.

Betty threw herself full-body on Vanessa.

They were animals — ferocious, hungry tigers, a matched pair, perfect partners — each one a slave to her weakness.

Betty was overwhelmed with the girl's energy.

Vanessa got on all fours again and demanded to get what she deserved.

Betty disappeared from the bed long enough to attach a black dildo to the hip strap she was already wearing. She'd come prepared, she prided herself on that.

Vanessa was wide open in front of this total stranger.

From Betty's crotch hung a thick black leather dick. Betty climbed up behind Vanessa and sniffed the girl's outrageously wet sex.

Vanessa felt the female's face at her ass, felt the breath against her cheeks. Like a dog in heat she pressed her ass back up against the female's face.

Betty sniffed for the scent that would tell her the doll was ready. Ready for the wild and free, fun and scary, out-of-control, roughriding fuck that Vanessa had come for.

Vanessa's scent was strong. Betty positioned the thing.

Vanessa braced herself.

Betty penetrated deep. She slid the leather dildo all the way inside Vanessa and pulled it all the way out. Then she saw how wet the redhead's insides were.

Vanessa couldn't suppress the smile when the stiff thing was again driven up into her.

Betty forced the dildo in, burying it in the redhead, pressed the black thing as far up as the redhead would allow.

Vanessa took it all in.

Betty couldn't take her eyes off the girl's cunt. Vanessa's lips spread open like they'd been waiting forever for this. Lips hot to the touch, lips covered with curly red hair sucking on her leather cock. Betty tightened her ass and rocked her hips forward and discharged the dildo even deeper.

And still she took it in, Vanessa's vagina was endless.

With each thrust Betty built momentum, butting her crotch against Vanessa's ass, dousing her dick in the hot come she could see but couldn't feel.

Vanessa spread open to the driving dick and the pounding she was taking from behind, a beautiful brute force. She felt the blows, felt the fingers squeezing her hips, bruising her ass, shocking her cunt.

Betty rammed herself into the pretty bitch, pushed her down to the mattress, smashed the chip on her small shoulders to pieces, gave her everything she'd come for. And then some.

Vanessa had never been violated like this. The level of pleasure was unequalled. A consciousness-raising rush swept over her.

Betty rode the redhead, fucking the little fox's thrashing body relentlessly so that Vanessa's hips, legs, ass, arms, tits, hair, everything was moving to the music of this expert fuck. Betty couldn't hide her pleasure, it was written all over her sweating body. With all her female force she fucked the girl.

The giant tits slapped against Vanessa's shoulders, the black cock cut her cunt. Vanessa's leg muscles were stressed to the limit, her cunt dripped with come. She couldn't have been happier, couldn't have stayed quiet another minute. Finally, Vanessa broke the silence with a cry.

Sweating flesh slapped sweating flesh until Betty brought the rebel down to her belly, prostrate, exhausted and dying for it, begging to come.

Betty decided to set fire to the red hair once and for all. She put her hands on Vanessa's clitoris. Deliberately restrained fingers were like a sudden calm inside the rough storm. Betty released the girl into her radical arousal with such a sympathetic touch, such a kind caress, such sweetness.

The instant the dyke's tender fingers touched her, an orgasm tore off on a riotous rampage through Vanessa's body. It burst forth from the girl's very pores. She tossed her head from side to side. The high, the rush. There was no controlling her shaking limbs, no silencing the turbulence within her chest. Her muscles strained with the orgasm, her body writhed with its release.

No matter how fitfully Vanessa trembled or thrashed about on the sheets, Betty did not withdraw her fingers, would not stop until Vanessa cried *"uncle."*

Vanessa Noble cried it out. Twice.

It was music to Betty's ears, and Vanessa's.

It was so good, such fun — such good, clean fun.

Rebecca Rose

*I*t'd been many years since she had looked at her body. *After Nathan what was the point?* she thought.

She wasn't an attractive woman. She *used* to be when she was a young girl, but not now. She had wrinkles now. Her teenage breasts once pert were now napping, her once-firm thighs were relaxing, her muscles loosening, her skin turning to butter. That's how Rebecca Rose saw it. You couldn't tell her otherwise.

Nathan adored her body. *Emphatically.* He called it perfectly imperfect.

Once or twice Rebecca accidentally caught a glimpse of herself in the mirror and saw herself through Nathan's eyes. Saw the reflection of a thoroughly lovable little body. In those rare single moments Rebecca Rose felt pretty.

Tonight she needed to see herself from that higher, kinder perspective. More forgiving. She called it borrowing Nathan's eyes.

Rebecca was a shy woman. She didn't expect this self-examination to be easy. But she was forty-two years old today. It was time.

The house was empty. Her two teens were in summer camp, her mother condo-shopping in Miami.

It was now or never.

She locked her bedroom door. She pulled her desk chair to the full-length mirror. She switched on the floor lamp *and* the overhead. She wanted to see everything.

Rececca Rose breathed deeply and took her first real look at herself. She struggled not to stare at herself like some researcher. She struggled to stay close to her heart and far away from her intellect. Her mind would cheapen this encounter, label it voyeurism, and dismiss it.

This wasn't the work of a voyeur. This was, perhaps, the most important work Rebecca had ever done. Intimate and rich with implications.

She began. Slowly she surveyed her diamond-shaped face and sharp chin ... When she was sad or afraid she must have nuzzled that chin in Nathan's neck hundreds of times in their two dozen years together ... Her auburn hair that she wore long despite the trend, alive with golden highlights ... Her hazel eyes, which smiled more often than not, usually at her own private jokes. (Rebecca was famous for her jokes.) Her turned-up Irish nose with a not-too-discreet dash of freckles ... Her lips— Quickly Rebecca turned away from the forgettable reed-thin lips she'd never liked. Then slowly she forced herself to look at them again. No one told a story like she did. No one kissed as well. No one spoke with more conviction. Her lips had served her well. *Time to see them in a new light.* She brought her fingers to her lips, moist soft smiling lips, and blew herself a kiss in the mirror.

She embraced the unembraceable.

She turned her attention back to her eyes and awoke a memory, long suppressed. Her parents called her sister "The Pretty One." Rebecca was "The Cheerful One." *So, her body had not forgotten.* She stumbled on the pain beneath that memory. Three decades later it didn't hurt any less. Perhaps more.

Her life was living proof that that which she resisted had persisted. Knowing this, still she resisted feeling. Instead she ran her hands through her hair, there where she carried her strength. She wore her gleaming mane like a prize. Touching it fed her courage. She brushed the ends of her hair against her cheek, then broke into a smile and relaxed.

She smiled at her naked self in the mirror.

Was this guiltless woman really her? If Nathan could only have seen her now.

The roving eyes of this guiltless woman moved down to a safe, noncommittal part of her body. She stared at her petite waist and the womanly way it curved out into her rounded hips. Then, impulsively, the guiltless hands fell from her hair to her small breasts. She cupped one in each palm and with the contact came a subtle seizure between her thighs. She ignored it. She considered the smallness of her breasts in relation to the pleasure they gave her. Small cameo pink nipples capped the ends of them. Freckles for days. A wide cleavage. She stared down at them, then at herself in the mirror. A perfect martini glass–full. She'd measured them in high school when it was the fashion.

"A martini glass full of pleasure," Nathan had said.

She stared curiously at the veins beneath her Irish alabaster skin. These veins had always displeased her but she couldn't remember why. Now they aroused her. Her milky white skin, those tiny pale blue veins, the touch of her own fingers.

She pulled the desk chair close to the mirror, and sat.

Her hands were drawn again to her breasts. Goose bumps rose on her arms and shoulders. She traced the outline of a nipple with a fingernail. Instantly her nipple hardened, her posture straightened. She was encouraged to continue.

Her imagination beckoned her to close her eyes, fantasize, masturbate.

No, she would not close her eyes on the one night when the gift of vision had been granted her. She would be fully present.

Both nipples were rigid beneath her fingers and her watchful eyes. She'd never noticed how pointed they were, how much smaller and firmer when aroused, or the way her breasts rose and fell as she drew in deeper breaths to accommodate her rising desire.

How many other details had she overlooked? Or the better question: How many had she denied?

She licked her fingertips and returned them to her nipples. A marvelous sensation of wet nipples, cool air conditioning, warm palms, and dead silence.

She tripped on another recollection that her mind had buried but her body could not: the first day of eighth grade, and she still wasn't wearing a bra. She listened to the laughter of a group of anonymous boys. You sure you're a real girl? they howled. She saw herself bolt from homeroom.

She ran her hands through her hair and shook the memory loose. *Rebecca didn't want to feel the pain.*

In feeling it, though, she'd set herself free. The paradox and the freedom eluded her.

She lifted her breasts slightly and caressed the soft skin. Excitement joined with goose bumps and together they rose.

Her palms stroked. There was no shyness, no hesitation. Her small breasts were simply beautiful beneath her delicate hands. Each hand squeezed a breast, each nipple pointed upwards, each breath deepened, each moment made new promises.

For courage she ran her hands through her hair before dropping them to her thighs. Tricky territory. Rebecca's thighs had always embarrassed her. They were masculine thighs, sturdy, muscular.

But she saw new things with her new eyes. *She had strong legs because she needed strong legs!*

She thanked them for helping her to stand up for her truths in life. She thanked them for getting her everywhere she needed to go: transporting her from a new job in Chicago, to a new husband in Seattle. They never failed her.

She sent love to her unlovable thickset thighs.

The intimacy of her homecoming dragged her forward toward a greater intimacy.

She spread her legs apart, exposing the pink, dark beauty. She left her hands on the soft insides of her thighs and stared into the mystery of her own body.

This was the bravest thing she'd ever done. She'd never seen herself this way, never dared look. She was looking now.

How much had she missed in her life by not looking at things straight on, accepting them exactly as they were?

With her fingertips she spread her lips apart slightly and confronted the picture facing her, the pink passage that led to her deepest insides.

What did it feel like inside of her, there where she buried her feelings?

Time to go within.

Sitting on a wooden desk chair, nude, facing herself full-front with arousal written all over her and her legs spread apart, Rebecca Rose barely recognized herself.

Her own cunt had terrified her all her life. Now as she confronted it in the mirror it seemed ridiculous that she was scared of her own body. But it was true. She was afraid to see herself — her true self — for fear of having to accept herself.

Or worse, embrace herself.

Or worse, love herself. For what an awesome responsibility that would be.

Her legs opened wider in answer to this new information. Her curious fingers spread themselves out on the moist blanket of her cunt. Prickly hairs matted down with *her* dew. Lips slightly swollen with *her* sexual desire. *Her* pink pin dot of a clitoris that made her call out when she came. It was time to claim all that was rightly hers. Time to know herself, time to love.

She ran her fingertips along the edge of her cunt. Blood dove headlong into her lips. Tight, tense, and terribly excited with a quick contact she rubbed up against her clitoris with her index finger and thumb. She spread apart the rose lips of her cunt and unshielded the clitoris from its hood. She sat and looked at herself in the mirror exposing another dark mystery of her own body.

Rebecca Rose grew more naked by degrees.

A tiny little organ, such a small pink thing, she thought. She weighed the pleasure it gave her with its size. Where had she learned that bigger was better?

She brought her fingers to the pretty crimson passage. She put her middle finger atop the hole and let it slip slightly inside of her. Her fingertip disappeared within. She shivered at entry. The buttery glide inside surprised her. It was far smoother than she'd even imagined.

She leaned back in the chair to see more, feel more. She slipped her middle finger in further. Her other hand kept her lips apart.

With her hands at her cunt, her arms at her sides unintentionally pressed her breasts together. She looked at herself. Rebecca Rose looked luscious. Yes, that was truly how she looked.

How she'd always looked.

The gift of sight was hers.

She withdrew her finger and lay the cream atop her exposed clitoris. In tiny tender circular motions she moved her fingertip atop the head of it. Her back and feet arched with the contact. She stretched her legs out in front of her. The toes of her petite feet reached the base of the mirror.

Covered in her cream, her vagina enlarged its passage within.

She was blossoming, literally, like a flower. Rebecca Rose was ripe for coming.

She sat face-to-face with her own arousal and loved what she saw.

The fingers of her free hand continued to move along the length of her cunt, from the tip of it to the base. Each time it reached the ever-widening hole of her vagina it dipped into the pool of come.

The cream was being spread like good news along the inside and outside of her lips, the creases of her thighs, the triangle of brown hair, even up to her belly button. Moisture abounded. A single finger was replaced by two and together they disappeared within.

Within, where Rebecca stored old memories she refused to face, or feel. Her destiny depended on how deeply she could dive within.

What she wanted to find could not be found in her cunt, but it was a start.

Could she spread apart the lips of her cunt wide enough to go within?

One hand was inside her and the other kept her vision unobstructed. The air conditioning made her cunt tingle. She pretended it was Nathan's breathing between her thighs.

Nathan, who was no doubt applauding from somewhere in the Universe.

The pace of her slow hands never quickened.

She watched in wonder as the red darkened.

Her cunt could hold out no longer. They begged for pleasure. And what was this new sight about if not pleasure? What was self-love if not pleasure?

Her beautiful large thighs could spread no further.

Her beautiful large thighs. Rebecca reeled under the realization. If she could embrace her body exactly as it was, couldn't she do the same with her feelings? Embrace them by feeling them and by feeling them, free them.

With her feelings and her fluids permitted to flow freely now, the purpose of her new sight was done. Rebecca's work, however, had just begun. She would have to watch carefully the workings of her physical body for it housed important lessons, important answers.

Rebecca's kindhearted hands put subtle pressure where it was most needed now. She moved her fingertips to the tip of her cunt and began stimulating herself. Her clitoris cherished the attention and responded quickly. She kept the hardened jewel between her thumb and index finger and stroked. Her fingers took on a steady spirited rhythm. Her touch was delicate but deeply felt. All kinds of tingling were going on within the walls of her vagina. She felt it clench, contract. Her beautiful thick thighs were quivering with the coming. Her body convulsed. She twisted in the chair — muscles tightened, breath held and body doubled up — when the exquisite friction brought her the orgasm Rebecca Rose richly deserved.

Tonight was one of those enchanted evenings when one sees her life with new eyes, sees the tapestry of her life right side up, everything in perfect order and place, sees herself in the best possible light.

Rebecca opened her new eyes and realized she'd fallen in love with her mirror image.

Paulette & Anne

*O*f course, I tell myself, it'd have to be raining like a motherfucker tonight of all nights. And I mean, buckets full, sheets of it, water, water everywhere. The driver, poor thing, is holding on to the steering wheel like some old lady and here I am, killing myself with anticipation because I've waited all my life for this night and this experience with a woman just like this. It's a tight squeeze in the backseat with me and Paulette and the lust and sparks and the real fear that we might not even make it uptown to my place in this cruel June storm. I'm heartsick. I could cry. I calm myself, "Anne, dear, get over it, fast."

It's the kind of thing where I met this woman two hours ago at the downtown gallery opening of her nude black-and-white photos and there were a couple hundred people there, but really there was just me and her? *Blindfolded* I would've found the woman, which is really saying something considering I'd never been with a woman before, although I've always known that I should be and, one day, would be. Don't ask me how I knew because I couldn't tell you, I just did. Sure enough, it happened and thank god I didn't do my usual wasting-time-not-recognizing-my-destiny thing when it arrived. When Paulette Strauss first smiled at me and declared, "You're too adorable for words," I knew she was going to be my first female lover. After thirty-three and a half heterosexual years, my search for the *right* first female had taken on epic proportions, so you can imagine that tonight I'm floating up in the vicinity of heaven with this Venus de Milo incarnate who's got the iciest green eyes — which I take as a *personal* sign, a go sign, green being my favorite color and go being my favorite direction.

Paulette's flirting up a storm.

And much as my animal exuberance wants me to, I can't make out with her right here in the cab. I have to be true to my long-awaited fantasy which demands a far more memorable setting. So I ask for inspiration, and get it. I put some cocaine on the inside of my wrist and offer it up to her. And sure enough, she proves to be the party girl, all right. She smiles a great big beautiful smile right at me, which I don't have to tell you gives my stomach a start. Then she inhales the coke in two experienced, *yet elegant,* swift snorts. It hits her like a whoosh. "It feels sharp and cool," she says. "It feels gorgeous," she says. "*I* feel gorgeous."

"That's the idea," I respond, and sweep her bangs from her eyes, and run the white powder over my gums with my tongue. And go numb.

The rain's making a splashing and splattering racket on the roof. Its point is well taken: *so much moisture.*

I invite Paulette to talk dirty to me. She tells me something about herself that she thinks I don't already know. "It was impossible for me to wait for our first date to kiss you." She's in love with the concept of being my first girl lover. "Maybe I'm too impatient for my own good, Anne, I don't know."

"Compared to my not being able to wait until we even make it upstairs to my bedroom," I tell her, "you're pretty patient."

We agree that there's going to be some chain-smoking going on tonight. I start the ball rolling. Paulette leans into me to light my Marlboro. "Let me," she says, real sexy, watching me over the little flame until I'm lit. But I don't say, "My pleasure," or "Thank you," or anything, because the minute I notice the French knot holding her hair captive I resent the hell out of it. Her lustrous, long black hair would fall halfway down her back if she'd let it. I touch the twist and admit that, "I must undo this."

"Be my guest," she says convivially. Her full smile lets me know just how happy she is to be with me.

It takes me a minute or two. When I am done a miracle happens. With a profound sigh the driver pulls over at the corner of Seventy-fifth and Park Ave. Home to him is Canarsie, Brooklyn, and a man could have two silent heart attacks between here and there in weather like this.

I make it worth his while. But sadly his autobiography doesn't end there. So I give him another two dollars, as I'm not one to put a price tag on my freedom.

By now, Paulette's gotten out of the cab. She offers me her hand, *not* her umbrella. "Come into the rain with me," she instructs, giving my hand a tender but unmistakably persuasive tug. "Come."

I can see with my own eyes that her hair is already wet, so while I'm charmed and everything by her mischievous impulse, I think it wise to wait it out. But what I don't yet know about her is that she's the kind of 25-year-old who'll wait in the rain until dawn for her *yes*. Or until the dawn of the next decade.

"The water will wash away your evil deeds, Anne, darling."

The darling business was new and I liked it. "What if I don't want absolution?"

"Then you've come to the right place, sinner."

It sure hasn't taken long to learn some things about Miss Strauss: She's childish and spontaneous and stubborn.

I dip my foot, high heels intact, into the lukewarm pool of water. Maybe I was seven or eight the last time I was barefoot in the rain. I step out of the taxi and regress a couple dozen years. In no time we're dripping wet. Neither of us wear makeup so we lift our faces to the rain like the happiest little girls. Our trench coats are drenched, our wet hair drips, and tons of raindrops splash against our face and eyelashes. We're drunk, all right, on dewdrops from heaven. We're moist, we're lust.

I unlock the intimidating iron gate to the right of my brownstone. Excitement's masquerading as nervousness and my body is shivering. I am cursed with the kind of body that can't tell a lie. This is the closest I've ever come to an anxiety attack, and why the hell not? I'm *way* beyond my safe boundaries, for crying out loud, I've never been with a woman before! The Universe senses my need, and adjusts Itself dramatically. It sends counsel to me in the spirit of Anaïs Nin. She keeps it short: Honesty is the best aphrodisiac. Straight talk. I confess to Paulette that I'm a mess.

Paulette laughs that great big laugh of hers and confesses too. "I know, so am I."

She's lying, of course.

I lead Paulette through a narrow alley that opens to my secret garden. Lights, cleverly disguised, are twinkling stars, and a rich, sensual aroma like something ripe and sugar-sweet pervades the heavy, dark, wet air. A fifteen-foot moss-and-ivy-covered stone wall will soon protect me from the eyes of everyone but Paulette. And the whole thing's like a mirage amidst the Manhattan concrete. *Perfect, or what?*

I'm wishing I hadn't done the coke, or had done more of it, when all of a sudden Paulette pulls me — *not* into the comfort and shelter of the gazebo but to the back of my brownstone, into the alcove with barely room for two. I swear to god, steamy vapors seem to rise from Paulette's skin as she leans her full body against me and claims her virgin prize. A chill goes through me, being imprisoned by the rain and by the way Paulette pushes me back against the building staring hard into my eyes. And by the way she says, "It's time for your baptism."

Paulette's liquid kiss to my lips initiates a wave of feelings inside me. I'm pinned to the wall in this tiny little dry spot in the center of the pouring rain *being kissed by a woman*. And my heart's beating itself right out of my body and I don't know where my head is at. Paulette's open-mouth kiss is more like a caress, incredibly natural and easy. Much, much more than I'd fantasized. And the tip of her tongue as it slips into my mouth is ... thrilling. Thrilling isn't really the right word, but I can't find a word big enough to describe the sensations flushing through my body as I'm swallowed up inside this first girl-to-girl kiss.

The warm wind picks up now. The tulips sway.

Paulette's tongue traces a slow outline along the sharp edges of my teeth. I'm in a state, completely unable to disguise my terrible impatience which, by the look of things, will soon be taking on a life of its own. Paulette senses this. "Relax," she recommends, as if it's that simple, "I want you."

What I want, on the other hand, can't possibly be crammed into three words.

The rain stops at nothing and ditto Paulette. She kisses each damp inch of my face. She kisses my eyelids. Her breath against my cheeks comes faster and warmer. So feminine — such a turn-on, the way she barely touches my throat and neck. Her sweet breath and bedroom eyes. The way she teases me with her tongue. Everything about this female is so ... *female.*

A brilliant flash of lightning slashes the sky in two. I know how Noah felt. I press into my excitement and against Paulette. I feel her breasts and belly and thighs. Paulette's a troublemaker from the word go, guaranteed to bring out the worst in me, if tonight's any indication. I close my eyes. I imagine what Paulette's breasts must look like and I pray they'll be revealed to me sooner rather than later.

Paulette forces her tongue between my lips, which reads more like a conquest than a kiss. Her hands do their own thing beneath my trench coat — they find and squeeze my bottom and hold on. They don't seem to want to let me go. Locked in this embrace of death I'm sixteen again — cutting class, smoking cigs in the can, getting felt up. So I ask myself for the tenth time what the moral of tonight's story's going to be — is it sex? or more than that? or more than that? Solve the riddle, Anne. I can't; Paulette's perfumed black hair puts a strain on my brain. She holds me tight, tight, tight — her hands on my fanny, her tongue in my mouth. "Oh God, Oh God," I repeat like a broken record as my body negotiates for needs with this kissing machine. I rephrase the question. Is it *a* girl or *this* girl I want?

I'm giving myself a black eye with these questions I cannot answer because all I know is that what this delicate raven-haired beauty arouses in me is no polite passion. My body's flaunting its inability to control itself. I feel the honey between my legs. Paulette has yet to touch my breasts. *What is she saving it for?* Water's seeping through the leather soles of my high heels. The alcove's no shelter. The rain's really coming down now. I feel the thunder under my feet, moving up my legs, and I'm getting suspicious that maybe *I'm* the storm. So I grab Paulette's hands and lay them on my trench coat over my breasts and I throw myself into one hell of a kiss. It's rugged, rough, and uneven and Paulette loves it. "Now we're getting somewhere," she laughs, her eyes sparkling like emeralds. I strip off my raincoat, I want it out of the way, I want everything out of the way. I want to stand beneath the downpour of her sex. My mouth's an inch away from eating her alive. I want it so badly I can't fucking see straight. The cocaine's not helping matters any, either.

We're in a *big* hurry. We've got lots of ground to cover. The rain splashes everywhere. We struggle with the buttons of my blouse, then my miniskirt, then I undo my brassiere and step out of my panties. I'm semiliquid before the rain even touches my skin. I grab for Paulette's hands and place them back on my naked breasts.

"I'm thirsty," Paulette tells me, which makes perfect sense with all this water. She licks the raindrops spilling down my bare neck and shoulders, and she works her way down until her mouth reaches my breasts. The touch of her mouth against them is awesome. I don't actually *see* stars, but it's just a matter of time. Paulette takes my nipple into her mouth and closes her lips softly around it. Then she sucks. And keeps on sucking on them like they're going out of style. She's making sounds and saying hot little things like "What a perfect body you have" and "How good you taste, how good you *are*," and things like that. And I try and try to record every detail of this night but I haven't got a prayer.

Paulette's hands glide across my belly, her fingers dig into the tops of my thighs, her thigh moves between mine forcing me to spread my legs. Then she returns to my hard hurting nipples. She's not done with them. She takes one between her teeth and makes it disappear. Later, when she comes up for air, she says, "I don't think I can suck on your nipples without hurting you." Like I really mind. "I don't think I can control myself ... your breasts are heaven, they're *torture*." Paulette's lips and tongue and teeth memorize me like I'm a test that she's going to be graded on. She releases me only long enough to catch her breath. The notion of *pace yourself* has no meaning whatsoever to her. "I want too much all at once," Paulette apologizes, pushing my breasts together and burying her face in the fullness of me. I watch the storm slap at the rooftops and feel her breath between my breasts. I wrack my brain but can't think of anything more important than Paulette penetrating me and I tell her that. And she tells me that she needs no encouragement, only a clear path into me.

So I spread my legs. The request lines are open.

Paulette smiles and says something excellent. "The incense of you is all but indecent." My cunt goes wild over that line. Paulette dispatches her hands to hunt down the scent, and before I know it she has my pussy full in the palm of her hand, holding it like some buried treasure. Her eyes are locked with mine, her voice very serious. "Your lips are very hot, Anne." It's true; I'm pretty much a liquid feast if I do say so myself. "Hot to the nth degree," Paulette puts it, knowing full well this kind of talk's just going to make me hotter. She strokes my pussy, then separates the lips ever so gently and like open sesame they part for her gladly. She touches my juice with her fingertips, only she's acting like it's precious and there's not enough to go around? She brings her fingers back up to my mouth and instructs me. "Taste this delicacy." I taste. She follows suit. I return her hands to the fireplace between my legs. "Not to worry," she smiles, obviously charmed, "my hands aren't going anywhere."

Neither is the storm — it's showing off royally with an electric-blue light show and thunderous background music. However, I'm too distracted to do any marvelling. Paulette's mouth is right up against mine. Her breath's stoking the fire. As if I'm not *more than* ready for the penetration, for the unlawful entry of one woman into another. *"God, what're you waiting for?"* Sounding desperate is not my first choice, but this is an emergency.

"For you to say *pretty please*," she answers, if you can believe that.

So, after I say the magic words, her fingers slide inside me, *way inside*, and I catch on fire BUT FOR REAL THIS TIME. I've fantasized this moment a zillion times and still I can't believe it. I *really* can't. And she's staring clear through me so I don't forget for a minute that I'm with a girl, as if there's a chance in hell of that happening.

"I've got two fingers inside you, Anne." Her fingers fill me up or keep me from spilling over. Like long-lost lovers, a vivid intimacy sparks between her fingertips and my vagina. You'd think she'd been inside me before, the way she's one step ahead of what I want her to do. "Your cunt goes on for days ... so smooth," she reports wondrously, deep-sea diving in the depths of a cunt more dangerously alive than I've ever felt it. I ask for more and Paulette obliges with three long fingers that sink into me. *My vagina's corrupted on contact.* "I can feel you in my stomach," I report, while absorbing the glorious shock of her enthusiasm *with pleasure.* Her fingers are FABULOUS — they were made for sweet-fucking like this with girls like me. They slide in and out of me a HUNDRED times before going off on a tangent and rubbing my clitoris *redder than red.* Giving me the feeling that she could stroke my pussy from here to eternity without tiring.

I say, "There's nothing on earth wetter than me."

To which she responds, "There's no one on earth to witness it but me." *Don't you love it:* She sees my orgasm coming before I do. She shushes me and gets real quiet, focusing on her fingertips as they rub my clit into clit heaven. And then *she* says the magic words. *"Pretty please."*

All I hear is the rain when my clit loses it. And right off the bat I start crying. The orgasm is understatement personified. And apparently it's got all the time in the world because it's spreading the good word inside my body at a snail's pace. Inch by inch, from Paulette's fingertips deep in my vagina to my belly, to my chest, to my throat — there's NOTHING inside me that's NOT humming. I part my lips to release the pressure. Paulette covers my mouth with hers. She inhales my exhale. She captures the spark and swallows. "Oh, how I like you," she hums. Now we both resonate.

Paulette dips and bends me and rubs her body up against mine and rocks me like some love song that I could close my eyes and dance to forever. I sway to it in the rain, in the nude, with the question of what to do with her after tonight smoldering between my legs. And it's impossible, I know — a minute's passed and I'm STILL coming. I have to concentrate. *I'm coming with a female for the first time.* I take a moment to take it in.

I never imagined that when the time came my orgasm wouldn't even have to raise its voice to get my attention. I hear it, it's real clear: I'm home.

And so, with its baptismal work at end, the rain drizzles ... and just like that, it's done. And I mean really, just like that.

Olivia Wilder

*I*t is as if days are decades, seconds are centuries, as if the night, pissed about something, is spitefully taking forever seeing its way clear to the cool dawn. A freak July heat torches everything in sight. Sheets of sweat drip down concrete buildings; Manhattan at midnight is melting.

Olivia Wilder lets the phone ring for fucking ever. She's dead certain the female's home, just not picking up.

She's girl-crazy tonight and her girl isn't at home.

There isn't a girl she knows, or one she wants, that hasn't left town for the weekend. There's no one to play with, no way to escape the heat.

Holding the receiver, standing nude by her terrace sliding door, watching the late-night electrical storm, chain-smoking French cigarettes, she brings her obsession with her into this new day.

All night on a slow burn. It's like being in hell. Crazy from the heat. Crazy from needing a woman. Trapped in this furnace that is her apartment, with her need for a female burning like an open flame in her cunt. She throws herself into bed and pulls a pillow over her face and lets out a groan that sounds like a roar.

She knows sleep will be impossible.

Use the madness, she thinks. Write a song — it'll pay the rent for a month. Olivia feels crazy, not creative.

She drags a chair out to the terrace. She goes back for a silver bucket of ice cubes. Her cigarettes she doesn't need — her cunt's already smoking.

She sets up house on her concrete terrace, tonight a brick oven, twenty-nine stories up. She falls splayed across the chair, dying from the heat.

She dips her hand in the ice bucket. The contact against her cooked skin stings. She selects the smallest cube, slides it over her lips, sucks it in her mouth. Her ever-grateful mouth. She sucks on it until she swallows it.

A fresh frosty cube replaces the first. She runs it along the outline of her lips, slides it into and out of her half-open mouth. Olivia doesn't swallow this one. The cube in her mouth cools her tongue, soothes her throat. She sucks on it until it disappears.

Relief will have to be found in this oral intercourse.

With the cool tongue she begins licking her fingers. Her thumb, her index finger, the gold band on her middle finger, and then her middle finger. From the tips of her unpolished nails to her knuckles she generously wets the long fingers with cold saliva. Slipping her fingers over her chilly tongue, into her chilly mouth.

The living room lamp illuminates Olivia Wilder from behind. Like a spotlight.

So that May, the oriental woman in the adjacent terrace twelve feet away can see the scene. Without being seen. If she is perfectly still. May leaves her terrace, she doesn't want to watch. She wants to watch, she's uncomfortably drawn to it. May's ex-lovers — all her ex's — call her a prude! May returns, rationalizes her curiosity, calls it an experiment. And watches.

The next cube goes to Olivia's brow. A line of cool melting droplets runs across her forehead, pauses at her temples. The cube thaws fast against her skin. Drops of ice water mix with drops of sweat. Keen little lines of arctic sweat slide from her temples down her neck to her shoulders.

The frigid ice against her roasting skin is bracing.

Olivia Wilder smiles for the first time all evening. That's something.

She dips her hand into the bucket, wets her fingers, runs her hand through her hair. Pushes her hair back off her face and neck. Cold dripping wet fingers, wet strands of hair, hot summer winds all mingle.

Like show-and-tell. May can feel the cold fingers. But who can she tell, who does she want to tell? What will they think of her? She can't not watch. May thinks, *oh my, oh my.*

Two ice cubes rest at the base of Olivia's neck. Soft hail puts out the fire. Thawing tears stream down single file between her breasts, cooling her cleavage. The tiniest goose bumps form. Her nipples harden only slightly.

She withdraws her hand from the bucket. Her palm, cool as a cucumber, moves to her left breast. Nipples harden like cut crystal.

Cool hand cooling sizzling skin, not cool enough. Olivia's hand disappears in the frigid silver bucket.

Olivia rubs the cold cubes between her palms. Liquid cold hands sweep across her breasts.

A single cube rests on each nipple. Her nipples might perish with the cold, but the Wilder woman will survive.

Olivia's nipples freeze. Good. It takes her mind off girls.

Fingertips to her lips, she tongue-kisses them, returns them to her breasts.

Wet and cold and hard and happy.

She pinches, makes them harder. Cool hands cup her B-cup breasts.

Wet in places where the ice has yet to touch.

Uneasy excitement arouses and disquiets poor May. She feels attracted, repelled, embarrassed, mixed up. She leaves the terrace, but stops short. May watches from inside glass doors.

The liquid chill is spread all over the breasts. Her breasts are the best. Can't give them enough attention to suit her. Olivia makes love to them.

Eventually she moves on.

Winter ice is slid along the summer skin of her abdomen, her lower belly, tops of her thighs. One chilled palm per thigh, she spreads her legs apart.

Shaved, oiled, glistening pussy steals the spotlight. The Wilder hands know the Wilder body inside out. Ice along a second set of vulnerable lips. Slippery lips. Bare lips. Cold cream lips beneath fingertips. A glacial cube cuts like glass against the thin pink lips. Stings the tender sweethearts. Up and down the fragile things. Cold, very cold. Violently refreshing.

May is wrong. Her ex is right. She cannot bear this hot woman nor her cold recreation. The experiment is complete. She goes into hiding in her apartment, but again stops short. Sliding glass doors stay open.

Intentionally, fingers slip. Clumsy fingers drop the cube against the vagina. Deep freeze. She pushes it inside. Ice-cold ice as cold as ice inside her cunt. Numbing herself in the name of pleasure. Secretly, severely invigorating.

Internal refrigeration within the walls of her vagina. Ice cold clashes with hot heat. Feels like hell on ice.

Olivia Wilder forgets the girls, the heat.

Behind the ice comes two cool Wilder fingers. Two cool Wilder fingers push the ice cubes deeper. Fingers cold — now hot — push the icy sensation further in. She waits. It melts.

New cubes come.

There is a method: She warms the cube against the burners of her thighs, reducing it in size. One hand parts the nude lips of her cunt, one slips in the cube. Her vagina does the rest.

Olivia squeezes the muscles of her cunt. A sex trick. Out comes the cube, warmer, smaller. She lifts it to her mouth, sucks, swallows.

It's why the Wilder woman knows the Wilder woman inside out.

Tropical heat sweeps across the terrace still. Beads of beautiful sweat form on Olivia's brow. More sweat drips down her spine, some pools on the chair below her ass.

The white woman's shaved cunt grows accustomed to the cruel cold. It can take two cubes inside, maybe more.

May returns to the terrace at odds with the irreconcilable push and pull, yes and no. She is aroused but isn't, she watches but doesn't.

Olivia's fingers press down on her clitoris. A tiny live coal sparking. She's working up to something: Two new cubes get rubbed against her pussy, sweat down to the right size, get slid inside. One hand grasps the back of the chair to steady herself. Crisp cool fingers sans ice slide against the shaved skin of her cunt. Unsparing slowness. Fingers dip in the ice, fingers harvest the cream, spread the desire to the few remaining dry folds. Hands moving like shallow baby breaths breathing arousal into the darkest flesh. Fingernails tease the sensitive shaved skin.

Olivia takes possession of her overheated self.

So does May, the woman divided. She goes inside, draws the blinds, locks the glass doors behind her, leans up against them, and masturbates.

Between Olivia's thighs sweltering summer winds whisper things, heat licks at her like a woman.

Hands to ice, then hands to cunt, fingers to ice, then fingers to vagina ... Palm to ice, then palm to clitoris ... They are exquisite sensations and Olivia celebrates them by feeding the fire. In little circles she surrounds her clitoris with cool caresses. She brings ice to the stiff clit and rubs until it smokes. The heat is oppressive, the arousal worse. Her fingers fan the flames. She inhales the fumes of her sexual inferno. No ice will cool her there. Nothing will stop her from rubbing, no ice will cool down the rising erotic eruption.

Her hot fingers go for the ice anyway.

Come, her cunt calls to her. *Come,* it calls. The base of her palm rubs nonstop against the tiny radiator in circles, larger and larger circles until she does as she's told and comes.

The seat of Olivia's chair beneath her ass is soaked.

Morning is hours away. She can sleep, she can write. The pressure is off. She will make it to dawn without a woman.

Alyson Publications publishes a wide variety of books with gay and lesbian themes. For a free catalog, or to be placed on our mailing list, please write to:
Alyson Publications
40 Plympton St.
Boston, Mass. 02118
Indicate whether you are interested in books for lesbians, for gay men, or both.